Dan Glaubke

Carol —
thanks for help!
Dan Glaubke

Taylor Lowe is a creative director of a
Chicago advertising agency.
Gwen Savage is an artist on his creative team.
During their business relationship,
Gwen encounters a would-be rapist,
escapes, and shows up at Taylor's doorstep
in the middle of the night.
The safe haven she seeks
begins a new life adventure
for both Taylor and Gwen
and almost gets Taylor killed.
At the height of
their growing love affair,
Gwen suddenly disappears
without a trace.

Why?

The answer won't be found in Chicago!

This book is a work of fiction.
Names, characters, places and incidences are either
the product of the author's imagination or are used
fictitiously. Any resemblance to actual persons,
living or dead, events or locales is entirely coincidental.

Publisher: Six Corners Publishing
                    13447 Wildwood Lane
                    Huntley, Illinois 60142

ISBN   0-9789403-1-8
ISBN   978-0-9789403-1-7

Printed in the United States of America

SIX CORNERS

PUBLISHING

Cover design and photo images by the author.

Dedication

For Bonnadeen Mary Allds Glaubke

Love you kid!

...

One

Chicago - 1970

Why?

Today that curious question that invades our being shortly after infancy, and is with us until the end, is a headache for which Taylor Lowe can find no cure.

"Why? I should be having breakfast at Eli's with Mark and lunch at the Playboy Club with Anders. After 5:00P.M. I was scheduled to have a few drinks with Wentz at Ricarrdo's ... listening to his advertising fables about what's happening at Burnett..."

Taylor's thoughts are suddenly ruptured by a loud speaker as he hears, "United flight 247 from O'Hare bound for Seattle now boarding. Please have your ticket ready."

The announcement is greeted by relief for a large number of passengers in the waiting area. The flight is going to be leaving at least an hour late. Taylor has been cooling his heels for more than an hour and-a-half and doesn't like the idea that he is here at all. He's one of the of the Creative Directors of Kobecki Communications, an advertising agency, and selling creative output is a job for the account executive, not his area of responsibility. He's going to Seattle to make a presentation to the Corcade Paper Mills. Mort Cooper, the account executive on the Corcade business was fired yesterday; Ralph Kobecki, president of the agency, said, "Go!" and that's why Taylor is here.

Taylor, at age twenty-seven, has been with Kobecki six years. He got a job as copywriter when he graduated from Northwestern's Journalism School. He was lucky. He has been one of three Kobecki Creative Directors for the past three years. And the youngest. He is six feet, two inches tall, weighs a compact one hundred and eighty five pounds, has short cropped black hair, brown eyes, dark complexion and most women think he is nice to look at. He has a distinctive crooked smile due to an intriguing scar that runs from his left cheek to the corner of his mouth. The scar is the result of being checked as he played hockey in his senior year at Northwestern.

Taylor has developed a new Corcade creative strategy for its packaging division. Dirk Davis, the president of Corcade is very interested in the agency's work and one tough SOB. He is the guy that you have to sell if you want to keep the account happy and

Taylor is nervous. He has developed some good things and has been in the business long enough to know that it is the people spending the money who call the shots. At times a lot of good work goes down the drain because someone on the client side wants to flex his muscles and says, "Go back to the drawing board and try again." Makes no difference if there is ten pounds of research to back up the strategy, or if it has been run by a consumer panel that loves it, or if it has been tested in the market place with great results; if the client says, "try again," you try again.

Taylor has met Davis twice since being put on the account. The first time was when a campaign developed by one of his counterparts at the agency went down in flames and Davis let Kobecki know that the agency had only one chance at keeping the business. Enter Taylor Lowe. He saved the account with the *"Send it in a safe...Crate it in Corcade Corrugated"* ad campaign.

The new packaging campaign Taylor has developed is livelier since it is aimed at buyers of consumer packaging, not the fuddy-duddy factory shipping market. Taylor has magazine layouts, direct-mail examples, and radio spots checked and stowed along with an overnight bag. His meeting with the client is scheduled for 2:30 P.M. and the 9:00 A.M. flight, even though a bit late, will give him plenty of time to get to the Corcade offices from the SEA-TAC International Airport.

The only thing good about the flight is that Taylor is flying first-class. Kobecki insists that his staff travel first-class on all flights that take more than three hours. He wants his people to be fresh when going to a client meeting.

The take-off is smooth, the "ETA" somewhere around 12:30 P.M., Pacific time, and Taylor welcomed the flight phase of the trip. He now has time to relax, go over his notes and prepare for the presentation. He is prepared but wants to anticipate what questions he might be asked.

"Would you like coffee, a Bloody Mary, or a soft drink? Would you like a pillow?" the attractive stewardess asks.

"Coffee. Black coffee. That's all I need. Thanks." Taylor thinks the woman is nice to look at and carries herself well as she walks away heading toward the galley.

As the stewardess returns with the coffee, the plane is suddenly jolted ... a number of times... traveling through an unexpected air pocket. The turbulence lifts the coffee from the cup she is carrying and drops it on Taylor's shirt, making weird and bizarre patterns as it presses against Taylor's chest and burns his skin.

"Damn it! Damn, damn, damn it. Ouch and damn it," Taylor rants as he yanks his drenched and steaming shirt away from his body. In that same instant, the stewardess tries and fails to regain her balance and winds up sitting on Taylor's lap pressed hard against him.

"Oh I'm so sorry," she wails as she struggles to free her bottom from Taylor's parted knees. Hard to do with an empty cup in one hand and no place to put the other.

Taylor stinging from hot liquid then lifts the woman off his lap and joins her standing in the aisle. "Shit! Pardon me, but I didn't need this today. Do you have anything for a burn anywhere?" Taylor had luckily put his suit coat in the overhead bin so there was no damage there; his pants had been protected by his presentation notes, but his shirt and tie are a disaster.

The stewardess does have some ointment and stutters an offer to apply some to Taylor's aching chest. He declines the offer. In the cramped lavatory, Taylor applies the burn lotion and does what he can to repair the damage. The ointment eases the pain somewhat but there is nothing that can be done to bring the stained and drenched shirt and tie back to life. His overnight bag contains a change of underwear. No shirt. No tie. When he lands, he will have to cab it to the down-town area, before his meeting, to replace them.

When the jet lands at Sea-Tac, Taylor's shirt is still damp. The stewardess offers to buy him a new shirt and tie, and Taylor feels she is trying a bit too hard to provide aid and comfort. At any other time he might have felt like pursuing the woman, giving in to the obvious overtures, but not today. He still has a *"Why me!"* frame of mind and is concerned about the presentation.

After arriving at a Nordstrom complex, Taylor has an hour to buy a shirt, tie and get to Corcade offices ... about a twenty minute ride from the store. It takes Taylor, no fashion plate, about ten minutes to buy a shirt and a couple more to pick out a tie. After changing, Taylor is as good as new except for the redness on his chest.

He's relatively happy when he sees her: Gwen. Gwen Savage. His girl. The girl he loves who disappeared from Chicago thirteen months before. She's here. In Seattle. In Nordstrom. Heading for an exit yards away from where he is standing.

"Gwen! Gwen! Hey! Gwen!" Taylor shouts as he starts toward her, moving as fast as he can travel in the crowded aisle. She did not turn. She plowed through the exit and when Taylor finally reached the street, she was gone.

"No! No! Not again!" Taylor rants as he looks left, right, across the pavement and through a stream of passing cars, but Gwen is gone. She's gone. Vanished once again. Just as she had disappeared months before. And Taylor's heart aches once again, as it had ached that day. He stands there searching but there is not a hint of Gwen anywhere. For a moment he believes he might be mistaken. There are people that look alike at a distance. But there is no one that has a walk like Gwen's. You couldn't find two people with that distinct bounce of the hips, that sway, motion that looks as though she walks to some silent, captivating musical rhythm. Most male animals that notice that walk are usually hypnotized by it. It's Gwen, he's sure it's Gwen.

Taylor stood there dismayed and couldn't think of a thing he could do to find her. After a few minutes he hailed a taxi.

"Driver, do you know where the Corcade Paper headquarter offices are located?"

"Sure."

"That's where I want to go."

The I-5 Interstate loomed ahead and his taxi caught the last red light before the entrance ramp. As they waited for the light to change, Taylor saw her once again.

"Driver, forget Corcade for a minute. Do you see the red convertible in the right lane up ahead? I'd like you to follow it."

"The Karmann Ghia?"

"Yes! The red Karmann Ghia!"

As they headed north on the Interstate the driver said, "Do you want me to pull along side of her car to see if I can get her to pull over?"

"No don't do that. I just want to find out where she's going."

They traveled for twenty minutes up I-5, and Taylor knew he was in trouble. There was no telling where Gwen was heading. If he didn't get the taxi turned around he was going to be late for his meeting and without a reasonable excuse. Gwen was doing sixty-five and about to pass up another exit so Taylor had no choice.

"Driver take the next exit and head back to Corcade please."

As they turned back and drove south, the driver asked, "Why did you want me to follow that convertible?"

"Long story. I know the woman in the driver's seat. Wanted to talk to her. We used to date. She disappeared without letting me know where she was moving to. Left without a word or forwarding address."

"You're not from Seattle?"

"No. Chicago."

When the cab reached Corcade, the driver leaned over the seat, looked at Taylor and said, "You don't have any idea where she was going do you?"

"No."

"Well I have her plate number, and the car was purchased in Mt. Vernon, about sixty miles north. The dealer is Harper Volkswagen. That's the name that was plastered on the trunk. The dealer should be able to help you locate her if you come up with a good story or pay someone off. They would have a record of the sale and the plate number on file. My name is Mike Danna. If the dealer won't cooperate, give me a call." With that the driver ripped off a piece of paper from a pad and handed it to Taylor. The paper had a license number on it and Mike Danna's phone number.

As Taylor gathered his bag and presentation, he said, "I ... I don't know how to thank you. You are a genius. Here's twenty bucks and thanks. You don't know how much this means to me."

"Well, you don't look like a nut. I'm taking a chance that you're not. I'm a cop and drive the cab for extra income. Thanks for the twenty. Let me know if you need more help."

Two

Taylor's presentation went much better than he expected. The conference room had been filled with Corcade people: President, Corporate Communications Manager, Sales Manager, Vice President of Research and Development, Manager of Human Relations, and a half dozen others.

Taylor's presentation positioned Corcade as an innovator with special capabilities, able to take a consumer product and help with package design in ways that were unusual. Unusual in regard to graphics, container construction, and the psychological aspects of container impact on the consumer. All the pieces of the creative samples incorporated a slogan:

Motivate people and market more ...
with Corcade Packaging

Taylor explained that most big consumer product manufacturers do their own package design and psychological testing. Since Corcade concentrated its sales efforts on smaller companies, providing services beyond what is normally expected would give Corcade a salable advantage.

Packaging that motivates consumers to buy is what Corcade was all about. In addition to trade paper ads and radio spots, Taylor presented an unusual direct-mail campaign. It consisted of a series of mailings that included an HO model railroad car as an attention getter. Four basic freight cars would be sent during a four week cycle with appropriate sales material.

"When a caboose arrives at the end of the fifth week," Taylor explained, "the message would tell the buyer that the power behind packaging excellence is ready to serve him. It would prod the buyer to call the Corcade Representative in for a meeting. The incentive being that the representative would bring in an HO engine to complete the train package and demonstrate how Corcade can provide dynamic packaging power for the recipient's marketing thrust."

The Corcade Sales Manager interrupted Taylor at this point and said, "That campaign would cost a fortune. We have sixty sales reps out there and potential target companies number at least a couple thousand."

Taylor was ready for this one saying, "We aren't suggesting implementing this to all regions until the concept is tested. We would like you to start the campaign with your smallest regional office. That's controllable and we can find out quickly how cost effective the campaign is without a major investment in time and money."

The sales manager said, "You think buyers are waiting breathlessly for HO train sets?"

Taylor answered, "No. We believe that older buyers will respond because they have a grandchild, or young relative who would like a train set, and younger buyers might have children, a nephew or niece that would be happy receiving a gift like this. Anyone can buy an engine on their own of course, but we think the campaign will produce positive results quickly. The idea is to get reps in to see potential customers.

"You know your representatives aren't making cold calls. We believe this campaign will open doors, get reps inside and make sales. I don't think anyone will be offended or accuse you of trying to buy business. The train is a small thing. And here's one small kicker. We recommend that the sales rep buys the engine for the sales call. That gets him involved. You are spending dollars to provide the rep with a prospect, his investment will be peanuts if he can make a sale. We provide the extra push to get him motivated and behind the campaign. The basic train cars won't cost much. The engine is more expensive and won't come out of your sales budget."

At the end of the presentation, the sales manager was still skeptical about the direct-mail campaign, but liked the overall strategy The corporate communications manager liked everything and so did the president. Taylor felt pretty good, except for the nerve jangling happening of seeing Gwen. That had left him upset and worried. He had thought he was over feeling anything about her and now he realized that was far from the truth.

"I want to talk to you and Drew," Davis told Taylor as the meeting broke up. Drew Daniels, the corporate communications director, knew what was coming and smiled. Normally, no one smiled when Dirk Davis called a meeting. Taylor didn't know what to think. In the president's office, Taylor was told to sit and Davis didn't wait until Taylor and Drew were comfortable before starting to talk.

"Taylor, we don't want to deal with Mort Cooper any longer. We want you to handle our account and I've talked to Kobecki about it. That's why you're here and Mort isn't. Kobecki told us you aren't an account executive and probably wouldn't want the job, but said it was up to you. I like dealing with the guy who is responsible for the ideas and so does Drew. Kobecki said that he will give you an assist in media selection, research and the other aspects of account work, so it's up to you. What do you say?" Before Taylor could say anything, Drew Daniels added, "Taylor, Mort hasn't contributed much of anything as far as Corcade is concerned. I think you understand what we need a lot better than he does. We like what you have been delivering and you have a good grasp of what our business is all about. I think your presentation today demonstrates that fact."

"Well," Taylor said, "you won't be hearing from Mort any longer anyway. He was fired. I have to be honest. Account work isn't my thing. Creative is my niche and that's what I like. What I'm good at. But I do like working on the Corcade business and think it shows. Sure, I'm willing to give it a go, but it will take some getting used to." Taylor was smiling, thinking beyond Corcade. Thinking about Gwen. Thinking this turn of events might give him the opportunity to find her once again.

"Fine, then it's settled," said Davis. "Drew, take Taylor to your office and let him know what's next on the agenda."

"Right, let's go Taylor."

Settled in Drew's office, he said, "Taylor, we're busy getting ready for our national sales meeting. Two weeks from Wednesday, we're hosting our rep organization at Pebble Beach. We want you there to present the new campaign, and I think we can use your direct-mail gimmick to our advantage there. I don't know how you managed to come up with the 'psychology bit' in your presentation, but Davis has already booked a psychologist to speak about the impact of good packaging on the consumer at our sales meeting.

"We'll be unveiling some new and unique designs there, too. Your campaign ideas fit our marketing strategy to a tee. Make sure you bring your clubs; we'll be teeing up after your presentation on Friday. Plan to stay through Sunday. Dirk likes to play golf and you'll be playing a few rounds after the reps leave."

****

After leaving Corcade, Taylor found an Avis office and rented a car. He drove north to Mt. Vernon, but he found the Volkswagen dealership closed for the night. He drove around for a while and then found a local restaurant, and had something to eat. He was hoping that Gwen might magically reappear once again, but it didn't happen. When he returned to his hotel room, he stretched out on the bed and his thoughts went back to the beginning of their love affair.

Three

It was in Taylor's third year at Kobecki, that Gwen was hired as an art director. She had been working at another agency and moved to Kobecki for more money, better accounts, and a side benefit: the agency was closer to where she lived ... a studio apartment on the corner of State and Ontario.

It wasn't love at first sight; she didn't like Taylor at first. Thought he was flip, too easy going, trying to be funny at times when "funny" wasn't. Taylor thought Gwen was too uptight, serious, sort of stuck up, not friendly.

She was nice to look at, built nice, curvaceous, had a funny walk, beautiful brown eyes, brown hair, and a smile that could light up a room, but she didn't smile often enough.

Taylor found out that Gwen was two years older than he was. At first, they seldom worked on the same creative team. Professionally, Gwen felt that Taylor was too word happy. She thought a strong headline with dynamite graphics made a better ad. She would make layouts without leaving the necessary space for body copy to make Taylor mad. Then she would argue that he should cut words to fit her layout.

Taylor used words to motivate and didn't waste words or space when conveying a message. He didn't like long copy and used clipped sentences. He wanted readers to take action, and learn something about the product. He wanted to make something happen. He wanted readers to buy and try the product. He had a way with words and was good at suggesting visual approaches that worked.

When Gwen worked with Taylor, she would work hard trying to find better visual ideas than Taylor had suggested. She managed to come up with a few that Taylor grudgingly liked and changed his copy approach to fit. But, it didn't happen often.

It was in 1968 that Taylor was promoted to Creative Director, one of three on the Kobecki payroll. It was a year after Gwen had come on board. The agency was growing and Kobecki decided to have specific creative teams assigned to the agency's account base. Taylor's promotion came two weeks prior to the agency receiving an invitation to make a presentation to Hershey Chocolate. Hershey had never advertised, and it was incredible that the Kobecki agency was asked to make a pitch for the account. Kobecki did have a few consumer accounts, but its strength was in business-to-business advertising.

Hershey had given a few agencies two months to prepare a presentation. Each would be given two hours to present agency capabilities ... media approach, creative direction, research capabilities. Ralph Kobecki didn't waste time; he called an agency meeting and let everyone know what he wanted. He gave one creative team the assignment of delivering a new and fresh capabilities package. The agency needed a new brochure and slide presentation. The other two teams were to think up creative approaches. Kobecki wanted to see ideas in a week.

"You doing anything tomorrow night Gwen?" Taylor asked after getting the creative assignment on Hershey and leaving the conference room.

"You asking me for a date?"

"No! No, I just want to get together and start talking about Hershey. I have a meeting up north, and it will run until about four-thirty. I'd like to grab a bite to eat, talk, kick around some ideas. You have a date or anything going?"

"No. Where do you want to meet?"

"Ricarrdo's, the London House? You have any preference?"

"Taylor, Ricarrdo's is noisy and loaded with agency people. So is the London House. If we talk about Hershey, it will be on the street before we finish an appetizer."

"Oh ... yeah ... you're right, point taken."

"There's a Chinese restaurant on Rush Street

that's quiet, where we can talk without worrying about George Lazarus putting our ideas in his marketing column."

"Chinese? Well if that's what you like it's okay with me. I'll meet you there around five. You don't have to bring your Crayolas, I just want to talk."

"I don't have any Crayolas, Taylor ... I don't use crayons!"

"Yeah, yeah, you know what I mean. You don't have to bring anything; we're just going to talk. I know where the Chinese place is. It's on the east side of the street, next to Tony's cellar. Right?"

"Right."

"See you at five, I have to go."

Four

When Taylor showed up at 5:15 P.M., Gwen was sitting in a booth near the entrance. The only other diner was an Asian looking guy sitting at the back of the restaurant. The back was just five tables away from where Gwen was seated.

"Have you been here long?"

Gwen had a pot of tea on the table and was sipping from one of those handle-less little crucibles that Chinese restaurants use for cups.

"No, the tea pot landed two minutes ago."

"You know what you want to eat?"

"Yes, I'm going to have the shrimp with lobster sauce."

Taylor tried to flag the waiter down as he took a seat across from Gwen, but the man was in, what looked like, a serious conversation with the other diner.

"Waiter. Yo!" Taylor said a little too loud, but under the circumstances it wasn't disturbing anyone but Gwen. The customer didn't blink, and the waiter came on the run.

"Waiter, we'll have two orders of shrimp with lobster sauce. I'll have a beer, any beer you have that's cold. Gwen you want something other than tea to drink? No. How about an appetizer or an egg roll? Anything?"

"No, Taylor!"

With that the waiter left them and hurried toward the kitchen, and Taylor could see that Gwen was annoyed.

"Do you always interrupt people and order them around?"

"Gwen, the guy over there must be the waiter's brother. They didn't mind me butting in, ordering.   It will give the cook something to do."

"You were rude Taylor!"

Taylor looked at Gwen, didn't answer for more than a few seconds and then said, "Yeah. You're right. Sorry. I'll give the guy a big tip."

Taylor wolfed down the entire entree, rice and two beers. Gwen ate about half the food and asked for a doggie bag.

And they talked.

Taylor asked about her background. She said that she had majored in advertising design and after graduating worked for Montgomery Ward in the catalog department. As she gained experience, she started knocking on agency doors. Six months of catalog work ended when she got her first agency job. She developed her design style at that agency. She worked there two years before coming to Kobecki. She didn't say what school she had attended, where she was from, nor did she talk about anything personal in detail. Taylor felt that she was leery about telling him too much about herself.

Gwen found out that Taylor came from the northern suburbs and had graduated from Northwestern. He got a job with Kobecki right after graduating with a little help from his father. "My Dad is an eye surgeon and took care of Kobecki's cataracts about the time I graduated. The Kobecki family and the Lowes have been friends socially for some time." The fact that everyone in the agency knew how Taylor got his job only made him work a lot harder. His work ethic and creative ability is what moved him up in the organization ... up to creative director.

When they started talking about Hershey, Taylor called the waiter over and ordered two Hershey bars for dessert. Gwen rolled her eyes. The waiter didn't blink. He walked over to the cash register, bent down and took the Hershey's from the cabinet below.

Ideas don't fall out of a head like apples from a tree. Taylor and Gwen talked, scribbled, doodled ... made lists of what they knew about the product, the market, and consumer buying habits. They discarded much of the trite, obvious and frivolous thinking as possible, but not all the frivolous, as they bounced ideas off one another.

The give and take seemed to be going nowhere as they sat among the newly arrived connoisseurs of won ton, egg roll, and chop suey. It was 8:00 P M., when Taylor finally said, "Enough! Let's knock it off. Can we get together again tomorrow night? There's too much going on to tackle this problem during the day."

"Can't tomorrow night, Taylor."

"Oh. Okay. How about Thursday night?'

"Fine."

Taylor didn't want to hurt Gwen's feelings, but didn't want to spend another evening with chop sticks, saying, "Can we go some other place for dinner?"

"What do you have in mind?"

"I think you were right about Riccardo's, Gwen. How about pizza? I can get one from Uno, and we can eat in the conference room."

"Pizza is okay with me, but let's have it at my place. I don't want to be cooped up in a conference room after working all day. I'd like to be comfortable. Uno's Pizzeria is only a block away from where I live ... you can pick up a pizza. My place is a better alternative than a conference room or pizza parlor."

"Where do you live?"

"Ontario and State, northeast corner, 2nd floor."

Taylor knew the neighborhood, and knew just where Gwen lived.

"Fine with me. What kind of pizza do you like?"

"Cheese is what I like'"

"No sausage, olives, pepperoni, anything else on it?"

"No. just cheese, but help yourself."

"Well, I'll order a half and half. What do you like to drink?"

"I've got coke in the fridge, that's what I'll be drinking."

"If it's okay with you, I'll bring some beer."

"Sure. No problem."

****

On Thursday, after work, Taylor stopped at a liquor store and bought a six pack, then went to Uno's.

With cold beer in one hand and balancing a large, hot pizza in the other he managed to get into Gwen's building, ring the 'Savage' bell, and open the security door before the buzzer stopped. Not easy to do, but he managed.

Gwen's apartment was stark. She had a drawing board with a light and chair that sat in front of the large studio windows on the outer wall. The kitchen was to the right of the apartment entrance. There was an electric stove, kitchen sink, a few cabinets, and a refrigerator. A small table with two chairs sat next to the refrigerator. Fluorescent lights flooded the apartment with a bluish-white brightness. There was a twin size bed, night stand, and a reading lamp in the room next to the bed. Taylor figured the closed door, down a short hall, led to a bathroom. The inside walls of the apartment were interrupted with a few posters. There were two large cabinets against one wall in which, Taylor believed, Gwen's clothes resided. This is all there was to Gwen's place. She made good money and if she wanted more, she could have it, but she obviously liked "stark."

In Taylor's eyes, the apartment looked like a transient motel room. To each his own, Talyor thought. He couldn't very well say, "Nice pad, interesting place, quaint." or use any adjective that would be apropos, so he said nothing as he dropped the pizza on the table. The size of the pizza practically covered the entire surface of the battered wood table top. The pizza was still hot as he pulled it from the box. In Taylor's mind the contrast of the half cheese pizza vs. the half cheese, sausage, mushroom, green olives and anchovies pizza was a bit like Gwen's apartment vs. his place.

They didn't say much as they ate. Gwen ate a slice and a half. Taylor ate his whole half, and if he had been by himself, he would have belched loud and long after finishing his feast.

"Have you thought of anything we can use Gwen?"

"No, nothing other than a kid's happy face smeared with chocolate. The obvious. You know, giant Hershey bar graphics. You're the creative director, I'm just here to glamorize your brilliant ideas."

You can knock the bullshit off, Gwen, and pardon my French, but I don't have any good ideas at this point either. We only have a few days left before the first agency go 'round. The obvious tag line would be something like, '*Take a Hershey break.*' We can think of something that's a lot better than that one."

"Taylor, that has a lot of visual and design possibilities. I like it."

"That's too easy. We're the smallest agency in this contest; if we stand a chance, we will have to do something that's really different."

They were getting nowhere and when Taylor said good night at Gwen's door, he asked if they could get together again on Friday night.

"Can't do it Taylor. Saturday morning would be okay if you're not doing anything."

"Saturday is okay. Would you like to come to my place or work in the office?"

"Let's work here Taylor. It's more comfortable than the office and if we're going to do some rough layouts, this is better. Don't want to drag my drawing stuff around."

"Yeah. Right. Crayolas are heavy!"

"Taylor, I'm tired of hearing about Crayolas. Drop the Crayolas. I don't use crayons. You aren't funny!"

"Sure, sure, okay ... no more Crayolas."

"What time can you be here on Saturday?"

"Is nine okay with you? Will you be up by nine?"

"Yes, nine is fine."

"Okay. I'll see you tomorrow."

"Won't be in the office tomorrow. I'm taking a personal day."

"Oh. What's happening?"

"I'll see you on Saturday. Good night, Taylor." Gwen said, as she closed the door.

On his way home, Taylor thought, "Your place

may be more comfortable for you, Gwen, but it 'ain't' for me. I think she believes I'm hitting on her, but she's a cold fish that I'm not about to swim with. Taking a day off tomorrow and won't give me a clue. Wonder what that's all about."

Friday was a busy day for Taylor. He had a couple meetings with clients in the morning. In the afternoon he filled in for Gwen at a photo shoot that he hadn't planned on. This consisted of some long tedious hours standing around, waiting for the photographer to get set up, and watching while he fiddled with the lighting, polished the product, tweaked it, nudged it, bumped and prodded, poked it, and then went through the whole gamut of maneuvers once again. The actual photography took less then ten minutes.

Gwen had called in and asked if he would mind standing in for her. She had forgotten to mention the shoot when they were together Thursday night.

After leaving work, Taylor went to Ricarrdo's and bent his elbow for two hours longer than he had planned. Six of his creative peers were in the lounge, standing by the bar, where the characters of Ivan Albright's huge mural behind it, looked down upon them. The guys talked ad talk. About who was doing what and where. Taylor found out that a friend who worked at Thompson was in Bermuda on a shoot that was going to last a week. He was jealous. Damn jealous. Most of Taylor's field trips never went much beyond Milwaukee.

When he finally pulled himself together and left the bar, he decided to walk home. He needed the exercise and needed to sober up. As he staggered down State Street heading north he came up to Gwen's corner. Waiting for the light to change, he looked up and noticed her lights were on. He thought that maybe he should ring her bell, ask her if he could spend the night, since they would be working together tomorrow ... ask her if he might share her twin bed for a night.

When the light changed, he continued walking north to home. He walked past Holy Name Cathedral, across Chicago Avenue, and up to Division Street as the stoplight burned red as he approached. The 'not quite corner bar' of Butch McGuire loomed ahead, and Taylor could not pass it by without a whistle wetter, and another before going on. He wasn't counting, liked the naked lady paintings on the walls and didn't arrive home until two in the morning.

Five

Taylor woke with his head aching and the phone ringing. He didn't want to answer, but he wanted the lousy, nerve jangling noise to cease. As he picked up the phone, he realized there was some place he was supposed to be this morning. When he heard the voice, he knew where the some place was located.

"Taylor?"

"Yes, Gwen."

"Are you okay? Do you know what time it is? Will we be working this morning?"

"Shit. Double shit! What time is it?"

"Nine thirty."

"I'll be at your place in half an hour. Thanks for calling."

Taylor showered, dressed, and was out the door

in ten minutes. He hopped on his bike. Zipped down to State Street and headed south, with head aching, and his bleary, blood-shot eyes tearing from a windy city breeze in his face. He rang Gwen's bell twenty-five minutes later. He yelled at Gwen from the foyer when she buzzed the entry. "Will my bike be okay if I leave it down here, Gwen?"

She yelled back, "You better bring it with you!"

Taylor lugged it up the steps. When he rolled it through the door, Gwen said, "You rode that here from where you live? Where do you live?"

"On north Cleveland."

"Is that close?"

"Close enough. About four miles. You know where the zoo is, right? Lincoln Park? I live around there."

"Apartments are pretty expensive in that neighborhood aren't they?"

"I guess, but I have a townhouse."

"You own a townhouse?"

"I'm working on it. It will be mine in twenty-six years or so."

"I'm impressed."

"Do you have any coffee, Gwen?"

"I can make some."

"Please. And if you have an aspirin laying around somewhere, I could use that, too."

"Big night, huh?"

"Please, please make the coffee. Let's just say I made a mistake, and I thank you for calling. Sorry to have kept you waiting."

As Gwen walked to the coffee maker, Taylor said, "I came up with something for Hershey yesterday. I think it might work. Listen to this..."

"Taylor, wait until the coffee perks, and I find that aspirin you need."

Taylor took a chair from the kitchen table, moved it closer to Gwen's drawing board, sat, and looked out the window at the State Street traffic. As the sun filtered through the window and warmed his face, he tried to get his thoughts separated from the pain that mingled among them. Suddenly, without any warning, two hands were massaging his temples, manipulating, kneading, and soothing his aching head. He sighed as the relief coming from ten wonderful fingers helped disengage the pain he was feeling. The therapy lasted for more than a few minutes, and Taylor finally said, "Ohhhh, thanks. Where did you learn how to do that? Please don't stop."

"Never mind where, and I don't have an aspirin, but the coffee is ready. I'll be right back."

Taylor hadn't noticed when he walked in, but Gwen looked different than she did every workday. She had on faded and well worn jeans; her feet were bare. The sweat shirt she wore was two sizes bigger than need be and hinted that she wasn't wearing a bra. Her hair was in pig tails. She didn't have any makeup on, and her face glowed. Taylor thought she looked terrific. As she handed him a steaming cup of coffee, she said, "So what's the idea?"

Before saying a word, he sipped some coffee, watched as she slipped into the seat at her drawing board, and then turned to look at him.

"Well, I got to thinking about all the negatives we're surrounded with today. You know, cigarettes are bad, cholesterol will kill you, booze will destroy your liver. There are editorials everywhere that talk about how we are killing ourselves. So I thought, why not position a Hershey bar as a healthy alternative. I had enough booze last night to believe a Hershey bar would have been much better for me. And thanks again for massaging my aching head."

"Taylor, Hershey is chocolate, not a health food."

"Right ... but stay with me for a second."

"Okay, tell me what's going on in that throbbing skull of yours?"

"Well, here's the slogan ...

   ... It's healthier to Hershey and a lot of fun!"
"That's it?"

"Hey, think about it! Everything we do these days isn't healthy. Smoking, drinking, eating the wrong stuff. Everything we put in our mouth is putting us at risk. Eating too much chocolate is unhealthy, too, but we won't be asking anyone to eat a pound of it. There can't be a jillion calories in one bar of chocolate. We'll help sell millions of Hershey bars and make people smile, make 'em happy and guilt free. Listen. Here's a graphic ... six guys are sitting around a poker table, and they're all smoking but one. The one is eating a Hershey bar, smiling. He has all the chips. The other guys are losers. And the punch line ... *It's healthier to Herhey and a lot of fun!* Another: A man is pushing a baby carriage with his wife, and six or eight children are in the picture too, all of them eating Hershey bars... *It's healthier to Hershey and a lot of fun!*

"We could have a spread showing six guys sitting at a bar ... backs to the reader and no copy, but it is obvious that they are sitting at a bar on bar stools ... maybe have the bartender in the picture drying a glass ... and then when you turn the page, you see all six guys head on and they're eating Hershey bars with smiles on their faces, chocolate in a beard or two ... get it? *It's healthier to Hershey and a lot of fun!*

"There must be an endless number of situations we can come up with. Guys sky diving, gals and guys skiing, some situations where people usually looked stressed out, but a Hershey makes everything right for them. "Celebrity endorsements ... can you imagine big photo close ups of Warren Beatty, Dustin Hoffman, Paul Newman, Rod Steiger, Anne Bancroft, and Audrey Hepburn eating Hershey bars ... or sports heroes like Roger Maris, Bart Starr, Gayle Sayers, or Dick Butkus? The only copy line necessary would be the slogan: *It's healthier to Hershey and a lot of fun!* Maybe have a little chocolate smear in the corner of their mouths. This is a natural for print, billboards, TV and the radio guys should have a ball with this, too. The idea can be used easily in any market."

Gwen looked at Taylor for about a minute, thinking, letting her mind absorb what he had said and then got caught up in his enthusiasm. She smiled and said, "Taylor the possibilities are endless.   I love it." Gwen then went to work.   Taylor didn't have a lot to do other than watch Gwen as she deftly stroked rough after rough on her layout pad. As the time passed they discarded some ideas, tweaked others, agreed and disagreed and kept talking as Gwen made some tighter renderings. Pages and spreads started coming to life. Things were looking good. Exhilarating!

As the sun set and the day darkened, Taylor felt they had more than enough for the agency meeting and called it quits. They hadn't eaten lunch, and hadn't stopped concentrating on campaign possibilities since Taylor had outlined the strategy.

"Gwen we have more than enough, let's get something to eat. I'm hungry."

"I could eat, but it's getting darker by the minute and your bike doesn't have any lights. Don't you think you should be heading home?"

"No. I'll be okay. Let's go to Riccardo's and live it up."

"Taylor, look at me. Look at me. Do you think I'd go to Riccardo's looking like this? No way!"

"Well put something else on and let's go."

"I'm not going to do that, or go there, and you don't look all that great either."

"What? What do mean?"

"Well, jeans and a sport shirt will hardly pass the dress code on a Saturday night. You head for home. I don't feel like getting dressed to go out."

"There must be a hot dog stand around here somewhere. I could get some pizza."

Before Taylor could say another word, Gwen interrupted and said, "Taylor, go home. I've had enough of you today. I'll eat right here. Take your bike and head for home. Thanks for the offer, but I'm tired."

"Oh. Okay. I'm sorry."

With that Taylor grabbed his bike and left. As he peddled home, his ego dropped more than a notch or two, because he thought everyone normally found him irresistible and an offer to break bread with him an experience to be savored, remembered, and enjoyed. He didn't really think this, but was more than taken aback that Gwen had brushed him off. He rode his bike to a favorite neighborhood hot dog stand, ordered three to go and peddled home.

Six

The agency had been buzzing with Hershey activity since given the opportunity to make a pitch. The time had arrived for the first in-house meeting, and the conference room was filled with people, excitement, and curiosity. Creative team one presented an outline and rough layouts for a new agency capabilities brochure and slide presentation.

Since the agency would only have two hours to present its case the capability presentation would be brief, and Ralph Kobecki would introduce the agency's media director, research director, account supervisor and the creative team. The directors would provide a short monolog regarding their credentials and agency philosophy. The assigned account supervisor, Marv Harper, would go a step further and provide an overview of how the agency worked and how Hershey would benefit from Kobecki's capabilities. The creative director, the one who would be working with Hershey, would present the creative strategy and show examples of what had been developed.

Taylor's presentation was the last one of the day. Both creative teams had been super secretive about what they had been doing.

Harry Benz, the oldest Kobecki creative director, had a team of four, and when they unveiled their strategy, people in the room were impressed. The team's overall theme was "*Take a Hershey Break*!" The strategy zeroed in on Hershey being an "energy bar" and when a break was needed, Hershey was a way to refresh your well being. The idea would work well with office workers, factory workers, doctors, lawyers and Indian Chiefs.

When Harry had announced his team's slogan, Gwen had looked over at Taylor and smiled. She remembered what Taylor had said, and Taylor felt his credibility had gone up a notch in her eyes.

As Taylor made his presentation he was straight forward. He outlined the strategy and the reasoning of what Gwen and he had developed. He said the campaign mirrored what Benz had talked about in his 'Take a Hershey break' strategy, but Taylor emphasized the merit of talking about health issues without being specific and that Hershey would benefit from the tongue-in-cheek approach. With enough exposure, he felt, people would be mimicking the tag line in all kinds of human situations.

When Gwen's layouts were put up and passed around, everyone thought the "It's healthier to Hershey" campaign would give Kobecki a better shot at getting the business -- including Harry Benz. Taylor explained that a number of Harry's team ideas could be used by making a simple headline change. As far as Taylor was conerned, things were looking good.

Kobecki had made reservations for ten at the Hershey Hotel on the day the agency received the invitation to pitch the chocolate business. He beat all the other agencies to the punch on good accommodations. He also booked flights on United for everyone, but Taylor had vacation time coming and he asked Kobecki if he might drive and take some time off.

"Ralph, if we get the Hershey business, I'll be busy night and day. I'd like to take a few days off after our presentation. I'd like to drive to Hershey and spend some time in Amish country, and visit some civil war towns since we'll be in the neighborhood."

"Sure, but you have to be at our hotel the night before the pitch to practice. I've rented a conference room at the hotel and I want everyone to go through the presentation a few times, even though we'll be practicing plenty before we travel."

"I'll leave early on the day you fly and I'll be there about the same time you get in. Harper will have everything under control, and if something happens to me, Gwen can fill in. Harper and Gwen know the strategy as well as I do."

"I want you there Taylor. How many days off do you want?"

"Four or five."

"No problem. Just make sure you drive carefully."

****

As Taylor was leaving for the day, he ran into Gwen at the elevator. He said, "We did it, didn't we?"

"We sure did. You were right about the 'Take a break' business.   I wonder if one of our competitors will use it."

"Don't know, don't care. I told Ralph I plan on driving to Hershey. I'm going to take a few days off and see the sights around Hershey."

"Sounds like a great idea."

"You have dinner plans, Gwen?"

"Yes, sorry."

"Nothing to be sorry about. I'll see you tomorrow," Taylor said heading for the exit.

Seven

Gwen had a date with Phil Fraizzer. It wasn't one she was going to enjoy, but she had to do what she had to do. She had been dating Phil for a little more than a month, and she had decided enough was enough. He was a nice guy, but had some quirks she didn't like and tonight she was going to send him on his way. He had been trying a little too hard to get to first base, and she was tired of it. Yeah, she liked kissing him, but that was as far as she wanted to go, and like all male animals kissing just activated his testosterone. She had had enough of Phil.

He was a couple inches short of six feet, with blond hair worn a bit long, had blue eyes, and was nice looking. No Robert Redford, but easy on feminine eyes. Gwen liked the way he looked. He wasn't a man's man.

He had some feminine mannerisms. Not anything that would turn a woman off, but what a guy would find strange if he was around Phil long enough. The only flaw in his makeup were weak eyes. Without glasses he groped. Things were a blur. He was a lawyer. Phil had told Gwen that he had passed the bar on his first try without any sweat, worry or sleepless nights.

Phil worked for the prestigious LaSalle Street law firm of Fields, Farmer and Green. He had been working there for six years. The joke around the law community was that the firm should have been named, Green Farmer Fields, but no one joked about the firms account base which included a number of Fortune 500 companies.

Phil met Gwen at an art exposition. He had been looking at a piece of contemporary art when Gwen walked up and asked him what he thought of it. That led to a cup of coffee, a casual first date, and nature took its course.

****

The dinner wasn't great. The food at this French restaurant was always wonderful, but Gwen was more interested in telling Phil how she felt and going home. Phil sensed something wasn't right.

"What's the matter Gwen? Don't you like the Whitefish?"

"It isn't the food Phil. I've been trying figure out a way to tell you what I have to tell you."

"Which is what? What's on your mind?"

"Well, I think we should move on and it's difficult to tell you why because I don't have any specific reason. I like you, but that's as far as it will ever go, and I don't think it's fair to either one of us to go on dating. There it is. I'm sorry, but that's the way I feel."

"You have another guy you're interested in?"

"Well, I have been seeing another guy," Gwen said ... thinking that the Pizza and Chinese with Taylor was a stretch, but not a total fabrication. Yeah, it was a lie, but she thought it might make things easier. "I'm sorry, but I hope you understand."

Phil was seething on the inside but managed to stay calm. "So this is it. I thought we were on track to a more permanent type relationship. What can I do to change your mind?"

"Phil, can't we just be friends and leave it at that?"

"Well, I don't want to leave it at that, but ... let's get out of here, okay!"

Gwen sensed the edge in Phil's voice and was more than happy to leave. So they passed on dessert, left the Chez Paul, and walked to Gwen's place, just a few blocks away. It had started to rain. They didn't talk on the walk, and when they reached the door, Phil acted hurt and insisted on walking her to her door for a "Good-by kiss." She resisted. He insisted. It wasn't much of a kiss, and then he left. Gwen was greatly relieved that the night was over.

But it was far from being over.

Gwen didn't realize that Phil knew where she had hidden a spare key to her apartment. He had been with her when she had inadvertently left her keys in the office and retrieved the spare in a convenient yet un-suspecting niche just inside the apartment's security door. It was on their third date. She rang a neighbor's bell for entry, picked up her key without thinking about Phil and that was that. The key was the reason Phil had insisted on walking Gwen to her door. On his way out, he took it.

****

Gwen had never suspected that Phil was a text book psycho. Unknown to her, he had lived through domestic violence and sexual abuse and was a killer at age 16. His father had abandoned his mother shortly before he was born. His mother then remarried and the man she thought would be the answer to her prayers turned out to be an abusive drunk. His mother had given up trying to find a way out of her dilemma. She surrendered to hopelessness and wore her scars and bruises as badges of futility.

One night, after being cruelly beaten, Phil waited for his drunken father to pass out and his mother to go to sleep. He then entered their bedroom with a baseball bat and deepened their slumber. He then lit a long candle in their bed room. Then blew out the pilot lights on the stove, oven and water heater and opened all the gas cotrols, shut all the windows, locked the front door and went outside and waited. As time dragged on, Phil thought his plan wasn't working. Then the house blew and fire enveloped every inch of what had been the rundown hovel that had been his home.

His stepfather and mother were burned beyond recognition. There was nothing left of the home. He told the police that his drunken father had beaten him and locked him in the garage for the night. When the house exploded, Phil said he had broken a garage window in order to escape. He had blackened eyes, a cut lip, scratches, scrapes and torn clothes to prove the point and the police thought he was telling it as it happened.

He was then placed in a foster home. There he was abused once again, but sexually, not beaten. The man of the house was well to do, his wife oblivious to her husband's proclivity for young boys. Old Mr. Morriane told Phil that he would pay for his college education if he kept his mouth shut and cooperated. He cooperated. And when Mr. Morraine was out of town on business, Phil obliged Mrs. Morraine's proclivity for young boys as well. When Phil graduated from high school, Mr. Morraine was true to his word. He not only gave Phil a college education, but paid his way through law school, too. Phil was intelligent, and a good student. Because Mr. Morraine was a lawyer, and had money, Phil thought law would be the way to have the things he wanted. He got top grades in college and in law school.

Women were attracted to him until they got to know him. His personality wasn't quite right. He talked down to people, felt superior to everyone, had opinions on everything and if you didn't agree he would try to intimidate. If that didn't work he would write you off. He had a temper that he fought to hold in check. When and if he lost it you didn't want to be anywhere near the man. After three or four dates, a woman usually had had enough of Phil.

Gwen hadn't caught on that fast. And Phil thought that Gwen was someone he would like to develop more of a relationship with than just a few dates. In his eyes, she was one of the best he had ever dated. Great body, great smile and she didn't try to compete intellectually. Seemed to respect his opinions. She didn't press him for information he didn't want to reveal. He hadn't taken her to bed yet, but in his mind that was a sure thing. He had thought it was a sure thing until she brushed him off.

****

Phil waited until midnight. He had been standing across the street from Gwen's building for twenty-five minutes, and when he had arrived everything, was dark. He felt secure that Gwen was sleeping. Gwen's key opened the security door as well as the apartment door, so Phil had no problem gaining entry. When he opened the door to Gwen's apartment, a hallway light provided a dim glow into the room. Gwen was asleep. Her bed rested about twenty-five feet from where he stood. As Phil entered she stirred a bit but didn't awake. He silently closed the door and waited for his eyes to adjust to the darkness of the room.

There was a chair next to the bed. He watched Gwen in her slumber as he took off his clothes and folded hem neatly and put them on the chair. Removed everything but his glasses. When he was naked, he slowly, and gently lifted and pulled the covers away from her body. He could hardly believe his eyes. She was bare. Naked. As if she had planned to entertain him all along and was waiting for his touch. He eased into her bed and ran his hand over Gwen's bare buttocks as he kissed her neck.

Gwen thought she was dreaming, having a nightmare, and as she awakened she began to understand what was happening and was paralyzed with fear. Phil was ready for her as she tried to move away and scream. He clamped a hand over her mouth and said, "Hey beautiful, it's me Phil. No need to be afraid or scream. This isn't going to hurt. I know how to make a woman feel delicious and I'm going to put you on cloud nine. Relax."

Gwen didn't relax. She struggled, but Phil was strong, and the struggling was meaningless. She shivered uncontrollably as he touched her, and the terror she felt took her breath away. She gagged. Her stomach turned. She couldn't think. Tears came, and as fear enveloped her, she stopped struggling.

"Gwen, I'm going to put you on your back. If you try to scream I'll hurt you, understand?"

She understood and shook her head. But, when he turned her over, her arm came free, and she hit him in the nose with every ounce of energy she had. His glasses went flying, and Gwen twisted, turned, kicked, elbowed, and moved every which way in a frenzy of physical exertion that forced Phil to lose his grip on her. Phil swore, balled a fist and hit her. The blow landed on her left eye, but he was no longer in control. Gwen managed to roll away and dropped to the floor. She started crawling, started to scream. The scream stopped abruptly as Phil dove on her. But, Gwen was then a mass of flaying arms, fists, and legs primed and kicking.

He was really swearing now, and trying to find a hand hold. He grabbed a fist full of hair, as he used his other hand to hit her again, but she kept swinging and kicking and finally landed a forceful knee in his groin. He lost his grip on her once again as he clutched his aching crotch. Free for the moment, Gwen leaped to her feet, and stumbled toward the apartment door. Phil groaned, moved toward her as fast as he could manage. His pain intensified as he moved and without glasses, everything was blurred, but he had to stop her.

Gwen didn't look back as she grabbed her coat and purse parked conveniently near the door. She flew into the hall and down the steps. Took the steps two at a time, managing to get her naked body into her coat as she hit the first landing. Phil wasn't far behind. Not seeing clearly, he stumbled on a step, and went down. As he picked himself up, Gwen disappeared through the door leading to the street. She was running toward the corner when the stop light went from green to red, and an empty cab magically appeared, applied its brakes, and she was safe.

Enraged, Phil went back into Gwen's apartment. He had envisioned a night to remember. It hadn't turned out the way he had planned. It turned out to be a memory that would keep his blood boiling forever. Back in Gwen's apartment, he got dressed, found his glasses, and in a rage methodically destroyed everything -- clothes, furniture, dishes, plates, cups, saucers, everything in the apartment that had any meaning in Gwen's life. As he broke things and littered all the pieces and fragments, his mind tried to figure out how he was going to destroy Gwen Savage.

****

It was raining. Lightning flashed, thunder roared, and wind whipped the rain into swirling sheets. Gwen felt the weather perfect for the nightmare she was having.

"Where to Miss?" the cab driver asked.

Gwen had gained her composure somewhat as the horror of the moment subsided, and the cab moved safely away from Ontario and State. Tears were still blurring her eyes as she choked out, "I have to find a phone book. I've forgotten the address. Can you help me?"

"Are you okay?" the cab driver asked. He couldn't see her huddled on the dark back seat but knew something wasn't right.

"I'm not okay, but will be if you can help me find a phone book."

"Do you have a name you can give me?"

"What?" Gwen answered.

"Give me the name of the person you're look-ing for. I'll call the dispatcher and have him look up the address. Okay?"

"Oh! The name is Taylor Lowe ... L-O-W-E. He lives on north Cleveland."

"Dispatch," the driver said into his radio, "Give me the address of Taylor Lowe. The guy lives on Cleveland. That's right L-O-W-E!"

Fifteen minutes later Gwen walked bare foot, through blinding rain, from the cab to Taylor's door.

Eight

It was around 1:00 A.M. when the door bell rang. Taylor had been in the sack for two-and-a-half hours, and had been asleep most of that time. He was groggy, disoriented, and thought he was dreaming. Then it happened again. The door bell. On the floor below someone was at the door. He quickly put on a pair of pants and started down the stairs to answer the bell that had rung twice more since he had gotten out of bed.

He turned on the outside light, looked through the sidelight, and found a woman standing there. She was turned away from him; he couldn't see her face. It was pouring, the woman's hair was plastered down, and her coat was soggy. Drenched. As he opened the door, lightning flashed and the woman turned.

It was Gwen Savage.

She was crying, and he could see her face was bruised. She had a black eye that was swollen shut.

"Gwen? What's wrong, what's happening? What are you doing here?"

He couldn't hear her answer, but reached out and pulled her through the door. The rain was intense, the wind bending the parkway trees, and Taylor wondered if Gwen had been in an accident. After closing the door, Taylor asked the questions once again.

"Phil!" she sobbed, "Attacked me. I was sleeping."

Now Gwen was sobbing and unable to go on.

Taylor waited. Waited until Gwen was under control again and said, "How did you get here?"

"In a cab. I'm ... I'm sorry, Taylor." As she shivered and shook, the tears continued to streak her face and she sobbed, and stuttered, "Taylor I'm ... I'm scared. Can ... can I ... can I stay here tonight."

"No problem, but I'm calling the police."

"No! No! No police.! Please! No!"

"Why? You're hurt. We should nail the guy that hurt you!"

"No!"

"Well, come on. We have to climb some stairs. You're soaked and we have to get some ice on the eye of yours. It's really swollen. Can you see okay?"

"It hurts, but I can see."

"Give me that coat. I'll put it on a hanger to dry."

Gwen had been clutching the coat around her,

holding on to it tight.

"I can't."

"What do you mean, can't? Give me the coat."

Then it dawned on him. Gwen was barefoot. She probably didn't have much on beneath the coat.

"Oh." Taylor said, "You're not dressed for the occasion. Okay, we can take care of that." He then put his arm around Gwen and guided her up the stairs. He walked her to a second bedroom on the second floor. He had her sit on a desk chair, then went to his room and pulled a set of old sweats from his closet. When he returned, she was still in the chair, still sobbing but the tears weren't flowing hard anymore.

"Look Gwen, you have to get out of that coat and give me what's under it. I'll toss it in the dryer. You have to take a bath or a shower ... has to be one or the other because you're shivering and soaked. We have to get you warmed up."

"Shower," she sobbed. "But, there's nothing under this coat but me. Oh, Taylor, I'm so embarrassed."

"You're kidding! Oh! I'm sorry ... you're not. Well, take the sweats into the bathroom and hand me the coat through the door. There are clean towels, wash cloths, soap, and shampoo in the bathroom. I'll see if I can find a toothbrush. While you're showering, I'll get some ice for that eye."

"Taylor, I'm so ashamed. I'm creating a problem for you, that you don't need, but I didn't have anyone else I could turn to. You're the only person I could think of that might help me out."

"It's no problem. I can help and it's no trouble, no problem, no anything. I'm glad you came here. I've got plenty of room. But, you're going to have to tell me what's going on and why we shouldn't call the police."

Taylor got some ice, wrapped it in a towel, and made the bed while he waited for her. The sweats turned out to be way too big, but she had rolled the legs up, clinched the waist tight and pushed the sleeves up above her elbows. Her eye was getting black, blue, and colorful in addition to closing tight.

"Gwen, sit on the bed and let me put some ice on that eye. It will help a bit, I know from experience. Played hockey, and I've had more than one of those."

"Taylor."

"Please, no 'thank you' words and if you insist I'll bring 'Crayolas' back into my vocabulary and we won't be speaking to one another any more."

She smiled slightly at that and sat there looking at him.

"Found a new toothbrush and a tube of paste. It's on the desk. If you need anything, I'm just down the hall. We'll worry about tomorrow, tomorrow. Can you tell me why you don't want the police involved?"

"Phil's a lawyer. How he got into my apartment I don't know, but if we call in the police, it will boil down to my word against his. I can't prove it was him. No one I know even knows we were dating. I'm beaten up; he doesn't have a scratch as far as I know. Who are the police going to believe? We had dinner tonight. Then I told him I didn't want any more dates. But I never guessed this would happen. I just want to forget about tonight and him."

"There must be something we can do. Have to admit, I don't know what. Anyway, you better get some rest. I'm just down the hall if you need anything. I'll leave my door open. Good night."

"Good night Taylor and thank ... good night," she said as she remembered the two words he didn't want to hear.

****

As Taylor dropped in bed once again, he wondered if Gwen was telling it like it was tonight. Her arrival with just a coat on was startling, to say the least. He couldn't help thinking she might have been coupling with the guy and when he started getting rough, she didn't want any part of it. Why else would she be naked? He couldn't get back to sleep. He dozed fitfully during the next few hours, and as dawn began to tint the windows with morning light, he heard her whimpering. She was having a bad dream, mumbling incoherently.

He went to her room, nudged her. "Easy Gwen. It's okay. You're okay. Nothing to be afraid of," Taylor said as she stirred. She instinctively moved closer to the soothing voice, opened her uninjured eye momentarily, then turned and went back to sleep.

As Taylor backed away and left the room, he found it hard to understand how any man could hit a woman like Gwen had been hit.

Taylor went back to his room, showered, then

dressed for work, made coffee and took a cup to Gwen. He found her still sleeping. He said, "Gwen ... hello," as he placed the coffee on the night stand.

She opened her eyes, confused at first, then sat up and said, "Taylor! Oh my gosh. What time is it?" At the same instant, the covers fell away, and it was evident that Gwen had discarded the sweats after getting under the covers.

Taylor, taken aback, looked away quickly, but it was a struggle. As Gwen covered up, Taylor said, "It's 7:00 A.M. Brought you a cup a coffee. You can't go to work today. I'll cover for you. Your eye is really colorful. Black for the most part. The swelling has subsided a bit. There's food in the kitchen. Help yourself when you're up to it. When I get back, I'll be back around noon, we'll go to your apartment and get some of your clothes. What size shoe do you wear? I'll pick up something for you."

"Taylor, I've caused you enough trouble. I'll call a cab and go home."

"In my sweats? Bare foot? I don't think so!"

"Sure, I can do it, Phil won't be there."

"No. It's not going to be that way. Don't go near that apartment. I want to be with you when you go. If the son-of-a-bitch that did this to you is anywhere near the place, I'm going to get a piece of him. Go back to sleep, watch TV, read the newspaper, I don't care what you do, but don't leave this place. I'm your boss, remember? It's an order."

"Yes, boss." Under the covers, knees now up against her chin, she looked forlorn, vulnerable.

"Do me a favor and smile. You look a lot better when you smile. No one will notice the black eye if you smile.   There's no need to look as if someone died. I'll be back around noon." Taylor then left, before Gwen could say another word.

****

Gwen got up a few minutes later, put on the sweats and went into the kitchen. With a second cup of coffee in hand she started looking around. The second floor had two bedrooms, with adjoining bathrooms, a small alcove with a stacked washer-dryer combination, and a large open area. Two big bay windows looked out onto the street. A small table and two chairs sat in front of the windows. There were no drapes or blinds.

The kitchen area graced one wall of the open space. There was a refrigerator, counter top where the coffee maker sat, a sink, and a couple of cabinets that housed cups, plates, bowls, glasses, some can goods, olive oil, vinegar, salt, and pepper ... things you expect to find in kitchen cabinets.

The third floor was a bit of a surprise. The whole floor was a big open area with book cases and a number of Art Institute posters hanging on the walls. On the ceiling above the posters were track lights. A huge desk, with a typewriter sitting on it, sat in front of the bay window that faced the street.   There was a park bench in the room and a couple of bean bag chairs that faced a big TV set. There was a wet bar complete with four bar stools and an expensive lineup of the best brands of whiskey, gin, scotch, tequila, vodka, rum, cognac and after dinner liquors. A small refrigerator under the bar was stocked with beer. Gwen thought it was obvious that Taylor entertained "the boys" here. Probably some girls, too.

It was the first floor that shocked Gwen. It looked like the photography you see in Better Homes and Gardens, Town and Country and the travel magazines. The ceiling was twelve feet high. Beautiful artwork hung on the walls. Oils, watercolors, and breathtaking photographs captured your attention, and Gwen found it difficult to move her eyes from one piece to another, for every piece was captivating.

The furniture was masculine, heavy and expensive. The hardwood floor was old, polished and added warmth to the setting. The living room area flowed into the dining room without a visual break. The dining room was big and held a table surrounded by ten chairs. There was a serving area, and hutch filled with expensive china. Off the dining room, came the kitchen. A modern kitchen, with a natural-gas grilling island in the center. Polished copper bottom pots and pans hung from a rack over the island. On one wall next to a huge refrigerator - freezer sat a double electric oven. The double kitchen sink was stainless steel and looked as if it had never been used. It looked like the kitchen, walk-in closet contained enough canned goods to feed a small army well for months. Gwen thought that Taylor must have had help with the ground floor decor, because there was so much contrast between

floors. She loved the place. The tour over, Gwen retrieved more ice for her eye, went back to the bed
room, and rested while she waited for Taylor's return.

...

Nine

Taylor had his workload well under control, and Gwen had a couple of things pending, but the due dates were still a few days away and nothing to worry about. There was one short meeting he had to attend, but at 9:50 A.M. he was finished for the day and out the door. Before leaving he told the switchboard that Gwen was on a photo shoot and he was going to join her. He would call in later to see if he had any messages. He then went to Victoria's Secret. He found a clerk whom he thought matched Gwen pretty well in all departments and proceeded to tell her what he needed. He told the clerk he needed a bra and panties. He said he didn't know what the sizes were but his lady friend was a pretty close match to her.

The clerk didn't blanch and said. "We'll give you a 34C bra and," then hesitating said, "well, I'll be right back."

He told the woman he didn't want sexy stuff, but he didn't want ordinary either. And, no, he didn't want to see it. Just toss it in a bag.

Then, he went to Saks. He wanted a blouse, half-slip, slacks and sweater to fit a size eight woman. That was what he got out of the woman who had waited on him at Victoria's Secret. She had said she was a size eight. He wanted a pair of size 5-1/2 low-cut shoes and some socks, too. He had found a young sales clerk who he thought had good taste and figured she would help him get nice things. She asked if his lady friend had a belt for the slacks. Something he hadn't thought about.

"How do you know it's for a lady friend and not my wife," Taylor asked.

The clerk looked at him, smiled and said, "Easy. You're not wearing a wedding band. Who ever she is, she is one lucky girl."

Taylor blushed his way out of Saks and with boxes and bags in hand, he arrived back at his place at noon. Gwen was waiting in the kitchen for his return. She was watching the news on his kitchen TV.

"Hi Gwen."

"Hi Taylor." She answered without turning away from the television. When she did turn, her eyes, black eye included, opened wide, and she raised her voice two octaves, saying, "Taylor, what have you done? Are you crazy?" She knew the bags and boxes didn't hold clothing for him.

"You can't go anywhere in those sweats. I want you to change and then we'll go to your place. Then after we get your clothes, we'll get you some dark glasses. After that, we can eat at some nice place. You are going to be dressed for it. At least dressed for it to the best of my ability."

"How much did you spend? How am I going to repay you? I don't buy clothes in the places you bought these."

"It's a birthday present."

"It's not my birthday, and we're going to take this stuff back."

"It's a bonus. The new Kobecki incentive plan gives wardrobes in place of money."

"Stop it, Taylor, I can't let you do this."

"Will you shut up and change? It's done. I'm not taking anything back. It's over. Done. Done, done, done! Change and let's get a move on."

Inwardly, Gwen couldn't wait to see what Taylor had bought. She wanted to kiss him. A thank you kind of kiss. You know, a quick buss. She couldn't, but thought about it. She tingled, couldn't wait to open the boxes.

"Do you have a hair dryer, Taylor?"

"Something wrong with my hair?"

"Taylor!"

"Yes, I have a hair dryer. I'll get it. The swelling around your eye has disappeared somewhat, but it's really black and colorful. Does it feel okay?"

"Yes, all I need is dark glasses."

"Should have thought of that."

"Taylor get me the dryer, and I'll try to hurry."

It took Gwen over an hour to get ready. She couldn't believe how nice everything was. She was thrilled. She had never had a day in her life when everything she put on was brand, spanking new. Today, was the day. She just wished it had happened for a different reason.

When she exited the bedroom she found Taylor waiting and he said, "Nice! You look great, Gwen. I have to admit my taste in women's clothes is exceptional. Does everything fit? Are the shoes okay, comfortable?"

"Everything is great, but I don't buy my underwear at Victoria's Secret. Don't shop at Saks, either. But, I really like the blouse, slacks, and the sweater is beautiful. Thanks, Taylor."

"Well, we need to get you some glasses, have lunch and then go to your place."

****

They ate in Old Town. Gwen bought some dark glasses. Really dark. Then they took a taxi to her apartment.

The apartment was a disaster. All of Gwen's clothes were in tatters, ripped to shreds, with the bits and pieces of material scattered everywhere. It was obvious that Phil had destroyed everything. Gwen was sobbing once again. There was nothing left that she or anyone could use. Not a thing. Without a word, Taylor led Gwen out of the apartment, hailed a cab, and took her home. He guided her upstairs once again, told her to change into his sweats, and to take a nap.

A short while later, when looking in on her, he found her sitting on the bed, eyes open but seeing nothing. He gently eased her down, held her and as some minutes passed they both fell asleep.

Taylor awoke, and it was dark. Night. Gwen was still sleeping beside him and his arm was aching, the arm he had used to hold her. He extricated the arm, got out of bed and headed for his bathroom. Then into the kitchen.

It was 8:30 P.M.. They had been asleep since 4:30 P.M.. He then called a local pizza parlor, ordered a half cheese, half cheese, sausage, mushroom and green olive pizza. When he woke Gwen up, she wanted a shower. The pizza arrived about the same time the hair dryer was turned off. He went to the bedroom door and announced, "Pizza is here, ready or not."

"Taylor, we have to talk."

"Yes we do, but I have to eat, and you should, too."

She didn't argue. She had two pieces and tried one from Taylor's side. Took one bite, made a face, and put it back. Made no difference to Taylor. He ate what was left of it.

As they ate, Gwen looked at Taylor and said, "I have to clean up what's left of my apartment and move, Taylor. I'll get a room at the YWCA until I can figure out what to do and I do have to say it once more. I do thank you. I'll pay for the clothes, but under the circumstances it will take a while."

Taylor looked at her and said, "Who is this son-of-a-bitch, Gwen? He's dangerous and should be locked up. He's a real nut case. I have a lawyer friend and he can get a restraining order, I'm sure, but you're going to have to press charges. We should go back to your apartment tomorrow, call the cops and give him notice."

"He is dangerous. I've found that out. I think he must be a schizophrenic or a psychopath, but if I ask for a restraining order, he'll know where I am, and if I press charges, who knows what he'll do. No. I'm not pressing charges."

"How did you get involved with him?"

"Met him at an art exhibition. He's a lawyer. He seemed nice, had a few funny quirks, but I didn't think they were strange at first. But, after a few uncontrollable rages due to some insignificant happenings, I knew he wasn't for me. I had only been dating him a little more than a month. Last night we had dinner, and I told him it would be best if we went our separate ways. He wanted to know why. I told him I thought he was nice, but I had met someone I was really interested in. It's a lie, but I thought that might be enough to make the split work. He grimaced, but I thought he took it pretty well. I was home by 7:30 P.M., showered and went to bed. You have probably guessed, I sleep naked. Can't sleep with anything on.

"Anyway, all of a sudden I came awake. Someone was in bed with me. Naked! Groping. I started to scream, but his hand covered my mouth and a voice told me to relax. That he was about to prove he was a better option than my new found friend. I knew it was Phil. I knew and I've never been so scared in all my life. He told me to relax and enjoy it. I fought with every ounce of strength I had.

"Finally, I got away from him. My purse and coat were right where they needed to be for me to get out the door and out into the street. Luckily, I got a cab right away before Phil could get his pants on and anything else happened. That's how I wound up at your door, naked as a jay bird, except for the coat. I still don't know how he managed to get into my apartment."

"He should be put away."

"Sorry, not by me. I just don't want to see him anymore. Hopefully, he'll just be happy with destroying everything I own and won't bother me again."

There was no sense arguing with her, Taylor thought, and he had made up his mind about the next step in his relationship with one Gwen Savage. The carnage of her apartment, her black eye and the saga of nearly getting raped by the 'nut case' had convinced him that Gwen was telling the truth and needed better protection than living at a YWCA.

"Okay. Now listen to me for a minute, Gwen. And don't interrupt. You obviously need a new wardrobe. You need a place to stay. You have to take care of what's left of your apartment. With the psycho on the street, that has access to your place, you can't clean up the mess he created. Not by yourself. It's too risky. He knows where you work. He's probably smart enough not to bother you there, but we don't know that.

"So this is what I am asking you to consider. This is strictly a business proposition. I've got this big place, plenty of space, no dogs, cats, just me. I might have a girlfriend or some guys in now and then, but I have no permanent attachment with anyone to mess up what's on my mind. I'd like you to consider renting the second bedroom. It won't cost you a penny more or less than you are paying for your apartment.

"We can get you a drawing board, chair, Cray ... ah, whatever you need for what you were doing work wise in your apartment. As you can see, I have a few bucks. I make good money. We can make this work unless you can't stand the sight of me longer than a work day. There's no obligation for you to do anything socially with me, unless you want to. We aren't dating, any new guy you latch on to will be welcome after we check out his background. That may take months after seeing who you were dating.

"Anyway, think about it. You don't have to say yes or no this minute. But we do have to get you some new clothes tomorrow. We are getting close to the Hershey presentation, and you'll need some sharp things for that day."

"Why, Taylor? Why are you doing this. You don't really know me. Why?"

"Because I feel like it. Want to. Lets leave it at that. Think about it."

Ten

Saturday morning, Gwen dressed in the clothes that Taylor had bought her and they went shopping. He took his Buick station wagon out of the garage, and they drove toward Milwaukee. Taylor had told Gwen he didn't want to take a chance of accidently running into her psycho friend, and it was a beautiful day for a drive. On the way they came upon a mall with a lot of factory outlets, and she wanted to stop. She told Taylor she could get by with a week's worth of under things, and when she was trying on some dresses, he told the clerk to double the order. Gwen insisted she could get by with three work outfits, Taylor made her buy a couple more and said she needed something special, a business suit for the Hershey presentation. He took her to a sports store and bought her some casual things. He bought some things for himself, too.

After the shopping spree, Taylor drove to Milwaukee, and they ate at the Grenadier restaurant. Then, he drove along Lake Michigan for a while before heading home. It had been a good day.

Along the way Gwen said, "Taylor."

"Yes."

"I accept."

He smiled, looked over at her and said, "Thanks. I was hoping you would."

****

The transition was easy. Taylor hired Service Master to clean up Gwen's apartment. Before the cleanup crew arrived, Taylor went over every inch of the place trying to find anything that Gwen might have left behind that had any value, sentimental or otherwise. He hadn't found a thing. He also informed the building owner that Gwen would not renew her lease.

Initially, Gwen was uncomfortable with her new arrangement. She wasn't looking for total togetherness with anyone. Now, she was in a night and day relationship, and it was hard getting used to. It wasn't the physical surroundings that bothered her, Taylor's townhouse was warm, and inviting. She felt safe, and secure. It didn't take long to see that Taylor enjoyed her company, but it took her some time to relax and enjoy her new environment. Many nights of the week she would be 'home' alone. Taylor would be working or out with his friends. He worked long hours at times, not watching the clock and returning home after the agency's cleaning service departed after midnight.

Taylor was a social animal. There were three guys with whom he played golf with regularly. They would come over to the house to watch ball games and drink Taylor's beer and booze. They would stay until the wee hours of the morning at times, talking about sports, politics, work, relationships, and more. They knew about Gwen. She had been introduced to them shortly after she came to live with Taylor.

One of the guys had asked her out, but she told him no. Nicely. And that was the end of his interest. She was spooked about dating, not comfortable even thinking about it. Still a bit wary of Taylor, too. He understood and made no demands on her. They did eat together a time or two during the week and enjoyed going to a movie. They went 'Dutch.' She insisted. He was okay with it.

Eleven

The final preparation for the Hershey presentation meant packing everything up for transport to O'Hare. Everything had been checked, double-checked, tweaked and rechecked. Only time would tell what the outcome would be. Taylor informed Kobecki that Gwen had asked for some vacation time after learning that Taylor would be away the week after the presentation. Taylor didn't tell him that Gwen would be traveling with him. When he asked Gwen to come along to Amish country, she thought people would talk and believe they were an item. He said that no one knew that she had moved to his place. They weren't an item, and he enjoyed her company. It was as simple as that. He would understand if she didn't want to go. It was up to her. She hadn't said yes until the day before the agency's presentation day.

****

Taylor was up and on the road at 5:30 A.M. He figured it was a ten hour drive to Hershey and he arrived an hour ahead of all those who had flown. The presentation went well. Taylor and Gwen shared the creative part of the presentation.

Taylor outlined strategy, Gwen presented the layouts that had been incorporated into a slide presentation. Some clever radio spots were played that ended with a musical jingle of, *"It's healthier to Hershey and a lot of fun!"*

There were questions. Some of the Hershey people seemed impressed. Some didn't. There had been a lot of laughter in spots during the creative presentation, and Taylor felt that that was a good sign. Ralph Kobecki was glowing and met with everyone at the hotel afterward. He was upbeat and thought everyone had done a terrific job. Hershey said they would make a decision within the next two weeks.

****

Gwen had told a few in the agency that she was going to visit friends in Philadelphia after the presentation. She told them that Taylor had offered to drop her off at the bus station in Hershey. So when they left the hotel together, no one batted an eye. Taylor then headed his station wagon toward Lancaster. He had made all of his reservations on the day he decided to take time off, and the first stop was the Lancaster Inn. As they entered the town there was a lot of activity. They had seen a number of Amish buggies on the road, and there were some parked in places near the Inn. Gwen didn't know much about the Amish, and that gave Taylor the opportunity to bring her up to date. He really didn't know a lot about the Amish either, but had read a travel brochure and that made him their tour guide.

"The Amish don't use electricity, own cars, or plow their fields with tractors. They don't have telephones. They travel by horse and buggy. They refer to us as, 'English' not 'Americans' and why that is, I don't know. Their clothes don't have buttons, they use straight pins to hold things together and I don't understand why. It has something to do with buttons being associated with military uniforms. For the most part they all dress alike and never wear anything 'fancy,' and with that Taylor's lecture was over.

"You really know a lot about these people. I'm impressed," Gwen said.

"No, that's all I can remember from the travel pamphlet I just read this morning."

When Taylor checked into the Inn, he asked for another room and was told that the place was full. It was tourist season. They had twenty-four rooms, and all were taken. Gwen was with him when he found out. Taylor asked where he might find two rooms and the clerk told him that he might try the Hershey Hotel. It was only about 30 miles away and they might be able to accommodate him. Taylor turned to leave when Gwen asked the clerk if the room had one bed or two.

"It has two twins, Miss," the clerk said.

Gwen then looked at Taylor and said, "Taylor, it's okay, let's take it."

Taylor looked at her, thinking that he wasn't hearing right. Her brown eyes were zeroed in on his, she wasn't smiling, but the eyes were giving him the assurance that she was serious and it truly was okay.

"Right," and looking at the clerk, Taylor asked, "What room is it?"

"It's room 100 at the end of the building."

After signing in, the clerk pointed Taylor in the direction he should go as he handed him the key.

Taylor then handed Gwen the key, and she walked toward the room as Taylor moved the car. Gwen had the door open and was waiting by the time the car was parked. As he passed her with some luggage in hand, he said, "Are you sure about this?"

"Taylor we've been in bed together before, and nothing happened. Nothing is going to happen here either, so it's okay. There are two beds. We aren't teenagers. You've seen naked women before, not that I'm going to wander around naked. I do have a robe. You know I sleep naked. If you turn your head when I get in bed, you won't be embarrassed. I won't be embarrassed. I know you won't force anything. I think you are a nice guy and we can do this. You won't try anything, right?"

"No, I won't try anything. Yes, we were in bed

together when you were upset. That doesn't count as being in bed together. I might not want to turn my head when you drop the robe to get in bed."

"Suit yourself. It won't bother me as long as that's as far as it goes."

"You're a strange woman to understand. Why don't we buy you some PJ's?"

"I can't sleep in PJ's. I've never slept in PJ's or a nightgown. Not since I was a little girl. I'm not about to start now!"

"Well, that's that then. Are you hungry?"

"Sure, we passed an Amish restaurant just before you turned in here. Let's try it."

They got through the night okay, and the next day Taylor drove the back roads of Lancaster. They looked around Bird-in-Hand, Intercourse, Smoketown, and other quaint towns. Places where it seemed time and progress had stopped and primitive living thrived. They passed buggies, farm land, and noticed that telephone poles and power lines were missing and the landscapes were beautiful. The smells of turned earth, manure and fragrant vegetation awakened their memory of exotic scents that no longer existed in their big city environment.

On Sunday they drove to Gettysburg, an hour's drive west of Lancaster. Taylor wanted to see the Civil War town, the battleground, and other historic places in the area. He drove to Biglerville, and Harpers Ferry at the confluence of the Potomac, and Shenandoah Rivers; and they enjoyed the Pennsylvania landscape along the way.

In Gettysburg their journey became a bit more complicated. Taylor had booked a room in the upscale Yankee Bed and Breakfast Inn. Originally, the inn had been a majestic home built in the early 1900's. It only had ten rooms, but every room had its own private bath, TV, and other amenities.

Taylor and Gwen had agreed that they could manage staying together in the same room, once again. There had been no embarrassing moments in Lancaster. Everything went according to plan with Gwen using her robe to get back and forth from the bathroom to the bed. Taylor checked in and carried the bags upstairs. Gwen stayed in the parlor area looking at all the brochures, pamphlets, and tourist 'come on' material about the wonders that lived near the picturesque hills, rivers, and byways of the area.

Taylor insisted they go the Gettysburg National Military Park first. They went to the visitor's center, museum, and walked around. They toured the battle-field and graveyard, then drove around for a while. For dinner they went to the Gettysburg Pub and Restaurant and it proved be a good choice. When they arrived back at the inn, they were tired. It had been a wonder-ful day.

****

"Can't wait for a shower, bed and the book I picked up at O'Hare. It's a page turner that's a lot of fun reading. It's a romantic comedy," Gwen said as they climbed the stairs, to their second floor room.

"I've got a good one, too. A John MacDonald book." Taylor liked the Travis McGee novels that Mac Donald turned out.

When they entered the room, Gwen looked at Taylor with her mouth agape and gasped, "Taylor, what have you done?"

"What? What's the matter?" Then it hit him. Hit him like a ton of bricks falling from atop the Hancock building. The room had only one bed, a queen size bed, and that was it. He knew if there was another room available it would be furnished in the same way.

"Damn. Didn't dawn on me. Saw it, but it didn't register. We'll have to go some other place."

"Where? Do you know of another place?"

"No, I don't! But, we can probably get a room in Harrisburg or go back to Hershey. Harrisburg is only about forty or fifty miles from where we are. I'll call." And with that Taylor started moving toward the phone on the nightstand.

"That's another hour or hour-and-a-half drive from here isn't it?"

"Yes, but the bags are packed," he said picking up the phone. He was irritated!

"It really didn't dawn on you that there was only one bed in the room?"

"No ... hold a minute operator ... it really didn't. I just dropped the bags and left."

"Hang up and let's talk."

"What?"

"Taylor hang up the phone for a minute."

"Why?" Taylor was exasperated with himself and just wanted to move on.

"I'm thinking." Gwen said as she shucked her shoes and sat on the bed. "What the hell, it's only for a couple of nights. I'm game if you are. You'll just have to promise you'll keep hands off."

"Hands off what?"

"Taylor!"

"Let me get this straight. You're suggesting we sleep together in this bed? You naked. Me in jockey shorts. And you want me to promise I'll be a choir boy. If I roll over in my sleep, which I am prone to do on occasion and a hand happens to land on one of your legs, boobs, butt, or anywhere it shouldn't be, you'll be screaming bloody murder. You'll wind up clubbing me with anything you find handy.

"Come off it, Taylor, we'll survive. You're making more out of this than called for. Relax!"

"No-way! You don't understand. I'm a full bodied, bloody lecher ... a horny, bawdy, randy, wanton, lusty lecher. I'm no choir boy. No, I don't think this will work."

Gwen laughed and after a few seconds said, "Okay lecher, I travel at my own risk. We're staying."

Taylor shook his head, not believing what he heard.

Gwen went on, "You want me to shower first or do you want to go?'

"I don't believe this. You're crazy. I'll be damned ... you go first."

When the hair dryer shut down, Gwen came out of the bath room, walked to the bed, carefully bent down and reached for her book that was on the floor, then dropped her robe and slipped under the covers. Taylor was reading, not watching her, but Gwen was watching him.

When Gwen appeared comfortable, Taylor headed for the bathroom with a fresh pair of jockeys. He showered and shaved. What was going through Taylor's mind and had been for the past hour would have had a psychiatrist jumping for joy as he contemplated writing a Pulitzer worthy article for his peers.

Taylor thought, *She's beautiful, nice, and fun to be with. Haven't made a move on her, but I've been thinking about it. Thinking about it a lot over the past week. Now I'm going to bed with her. She's as bare as she was coming into the world, and if I make one wrong move, I will have shut down any kind of relationship forever. At least I think that's what would happen. I just might lose my mind tonight. It 'ain't' fair!*

As he finished in the bathroom and came toward the bed, Gwen watched him. He was aware that she was looking at him. He thought, in jockey shorts, what you see is what you get. Almost. He knew that physically he wasn't bad to look at. He had played hockey in high school and college and was still in good shape. He worked out consistently. Pecs were tight, stomach flat. He was no Adonis, but he wasn't ugly. He knew a few women that thought of him as attractive. He wasn't a genius, and he wasn't dumb. He believed he had a persona that both men and women might admire. He didn't think he had many enemies.

What he would like to know is what Gwen

thought of him. Not a question you ask anybody ... wearing jockey shorts. He would like to know if his assessment of himself was pretty much on target in Gwen's eyes. He was in an awkward position. He was her boss. Her landlord. A shoulder to cry on. He was a bright, creative guy, but at the moment had no idea how to change his relationship with her.

He picked up his book, slipped stealthily into bed, careful not to touch her in any way. Tough for him not to do in the queen size bed, but he managed. They didn't talk. They read. They felt that conversation might erupt in embarrassing words, create a misunder-standing or produce an extremely awkward situation. Because they were both uncomfortable they concen-trated on their books. The minutes ticked, tocked, ticked and tocked and when 11:30 P.M. approached, Taylor's eyelids started to close. He put his book on the night-stand, said good night, and sought a peaceful night's sleep. Gwen then turned her light off, snug-gled under the covers, turned on her side away from him, and bid him a 'good night' as well.

It happened sometime during the early morn-ing hours. It was still dark when Taylor found himself on his back, half awake, yet with eyes clamped shut. At that moment not aware of who the knee belonged to that had just come to rest upon his manhood, or the hand on his shoulder. Conscious then of a warm breast nestled against his arm, then aware that his space on the bed had suddenly grown smaller. He was now awake. Wide awake. Turning his head slightly, care-fully, he realized that Gwen was still in never-never land. He could feel her warm breath on his neck every time she exhaled. He was paralyzed, afraid to move. He believed if he nudged her, she'd get the wrong idea and everything would be over. Not just for today, but forever. She would move out of his place and would probably look for another job. So he lay there. He liked the feeling of the arm, breast, and leg on his being. The knee was a bit uncomfortable and as long as the thing under it didn't come to life, that was okay, too. Then, again, the warm breath on his neck was starting to have an effect on him.

Then, Gwen turned and all of her warm, wonderful skin disappeared from his being. She was awake. In the next minute she skipped out of bed ... with her robe in her hand, dragging on the floor ... as she headed for the bathroom. Enough light filtered through the window to enable Taylor to see her, enjoy her backside, and appreciate all the contours and curves that made Gwen a very special lady in his eyes. What he enjoyed most was her wonderful bouncy walk. Her undulating buns and hips danced as she walked. He couldn't remember seeing any woman's walk that excited him so.

Taylor dozed off and when he awoke again, Gwen was sitting in a chair reading her book. She was dressed and ready to go.

"How long have you been up and waiting for me?"

"Not long sleepy head."

Taylor got up and as he picked out clothes for the day said, "After I get dressed we should pack up and leave."

"I thought you booked this room for two nights."

"I did, but under the circumstances, I think we should move on."

"No need, I slept okay. We can manage another night."

"You didn't ask how I slept."

"Didn't notice that you tossed and turned."

"I was afraid to move!"

"Poor baby. Was it that bad?"

"Not bad at all, especially when you rolled over on me."

"Did not!"

"Oh yes you did, and you know it."

"It was just an arm and a leg." Gwen said with a half smile, half frown on her face.

"You forgot to mention that beautiful boob that landed on me."

"No!"

"Oh, yes, yes, yes, but I didn't mind a bit, in fact I enjoyed it."

"Why didn't you push me away?"

"Are you crazy. If I had touched you, you would have thought the worst. You'd probably have given me a shiner, and I'd have had to get my own ice."

"Maybe ... maybe not."

"Listen. That bed's too damn small for two naked bodies that are nothing more than friends. There must be another room down the road that we can find."

"No, Taylor. I like this place. I want to stay here."

Taylor did too, but Gwen was the one who had to tell him that it was okay.

"Fine I'll see if they have a cot, and if they do we can flip for it."

"Come on. We can get through one more night. Let's get going; there's a lot you want to see, and I do, too."

If the truth be known, Taylor would have forgone the sight seeing of the country side for views of Gwen's naked landscape, but off they went.

They visited Sharpsburg, Maryland where the battle of Antietam was fought, by far the bloodiest battle in American history. Twenty-three thousand soldiers were among the dead, wounded or missing in twelve hours of fighting on September 17th in 1862. They found a place called Cashtown and had lunch. The Civil War tavern there serves a hardy meal, and Gwen and Taylor savored the history of the place, in addition to the food. The country side in their meandering was beautiful.

They looked and talked as the back road miles went bumping by. Taylor told Gwen about his youth, playing hockey, and why he decided to get into advertising instead of following his dad into medicine. He told her what it was like growing up on the north shore. Gwen was reticent about her past. She did tell Taylor that she was raised on a farm out west. She had always enjoyed drawing. In art school she enjoyed the challenge that print advertising design work offered. Her job at Wards had been a downer. She loved agency work and the agency work environment. She jabbed

Taylor with, "Loved the job until I got you for a boss!"

Taylor told her that her work ethic was great. That he was happy with her work. Happy that Kobecki put her on his team. Thought they made a great team.

"I'd like it if you made the copy blocks a bit more realistic, but other than that you really make your Crayolas work."

"Taylor!" she said as she punched his arm.

"Hey, take it easy, I almost lost control of the car."

"Yeah. Just think what the local paper would say, 'Hot hockey jock laid low by a weak wench."

"Now, you're writing headlines, too?"

"You're not the only one who has a way with words."

"Stick to the Crayolas!" He answered and grabbed her fist before the punch landed.

They laughed and enjoyed each other as they traveled down the road. Then the day darkened, and it began to rain. After eating dinner they got a bit wet when parking the car. Once in the room, Gwen told Taylor she was taking her shower first ... then once again slid demurely into bed.

Taylor was in the middle of his MacDonald novel when Gwen finished her book and turned off her light.

She said, "Good-night."

He mumbled, "Yes ... good night," and his eyes never left the paragraph on the page in front of him.

Gwen had been lying beside him for a minute when she suddenly and impulsively sat up ignoring all modesty, put her arms around Taylor's neck and kissed him. She gave him a long, exploring, and lingering wet and lust inspiring kiss. Then, pulling away and covering up she lay down, turned her back to him and said, "Good night!" once again.

"What in hell was that all about?" Taylor said, looking down at the back of her head.

"Partly a thank you, partly something I've been wanting to do, partly the end of a beautiful day. But, that's as far as it goes, Taylor. See you in the morning."

"You just took an awful chance, lady. I wish you had given me some warning. You wouldn't want to try that again, would you? I'm ready for you now. Boy am I ready!"

"Good night Taylor."

"Well, if you need me for anything else, I'm right here!"

Taylor was shaking his head and couldn't see the smile that Gwen had on her face. He thought, *"Good night? ... She must think I'm a eunuch."*

In the middle of the night their sleeping bodies stirred, turned, touched and Taylor awoke. For a moment, as his eyes opened, he thought he was dreaming. As Gwen's sensuous, naked body snuggled against his, he carefully began stroking her hair, touching her face. Her eyes opened, and she saw him watching her. She responded to the loving look in his eyes by kissing him again. Softly. Their second kiss of the night was just momentary pressure, not lingering or lust driven, but meaningful just the same. She continued snuggling against him as she drifted back into slumberland. Taylor was hard pressed to remain calm with Gwen's naked body pressed against him, but he too, drifted into sleep once again. When he awoke, Gwen was dressed, packed, and ready to go.

"Ready for breakfast, Taylor?"

"Ready for something."

"Well, whatever it is, you'll probably find it down the road."

Twelve

As they drove back to Chicago through Ohio and Indiana, they talked. Spent time learning each others likes and dislikes. Along the way, Gwen told Taylor she was afraid of getting too serious with him. She thought, but didn't say that Phil had fooled her, and she wasn't sure she could trust anyone at the moment. She thought Taylor was too good to be true. She had never met anyone like him. As they continued traveling, Taylor told her he wanted a serious relationship, that he had fallen for her. He told himself it wasn't because of her naked body. He didn't like thinking about that. No. Not true. He liked thinking about it. A lot. He liked remembering what she felt like ... snuggled against him. He told Gwen he liked being with her, liked being around her, liked working with her.

He told her that, he never had had a serious love affair. He liked some of the women he dated, but that was as far as it went. And the situation they were now in had changed everything for him. Taylor told Gwen he would be patient and would be there for her no matter what, but wanted her to know he wanted her. He wanted more than a good night kiss relationship.

"I'm not ready for that Taylor. I like you. I'm taking advantage of you, and I don't like that. I should move out, but I don't want to. If I let you touch me, hold me, kiss me, it's going to be impossible for you ... and for me ... to stop. I don't want that to happen ... not yet. Do you understand? I'm asking you to be patient."

"I understand and I'll be patient," Taylor said with a sigh, "but I don't like it. How long is this going to take?"

"I don't know, but don't put pressure on me, okay?"

Taylor didn't answer and neither of them talked for the two hours left on their journey home.

****

Taylor was a Christian. Believed. He had been brought up Presbyterian, but like many young men had wandered away from the Lord. He knew he was a sinner many times over, but when he thought about Gwen, he was thinking that he better start changing his ways. With a number of women he had been dating, he had had a bam, bam, thank you Ma'am relationship. It was fun and games, but no substance. A few women had wanted more than he was willing to give. Because he was a selfish guy, he wanted to play without any responsibility attached.

Gwen had changed his mind set. Gwen was more mature than he was. Two years older and more in control of her emotions. Taylor thought she didn't understand his emotional makeup. He really didn't understand his emotional makeup himself. Was it love or lust that was confronting him? He felt it was probably a bit of both.

Gwen had never had a relationship with God. She thought that in the complex world, nature was nature, and for the most part she let nature take its course. Growing up on a farm, she knew a lot about nature. She wasn't a bad person, but she had been sexually promiscuous and lost her virginity at age 15. Then she shaped up and didn't go down that path much again. She was careful who she dated. Phil had turned out to be bad judgement, but in retrospect she knew she wouldn't be living with Taylor if it hadn't been for Phil. And she did like what was happening in her life since she moved in with him. Yet, it seemed things were moving too fast.

After unpacking the bags when they reached home, they sat in the second floor kitchen and made small talk until Gwen confronted Taylor with, "Taylor we can't go on working together."

"What do you mean, why not?"

"Everyone will guess or know we're involved in short order."

"Don't be silly."

"Taylor, there are going to be times when you look at me that will tell we're involved. Affection is hard to hide. We'll wind up all over each other, and someone will see it and talk."

"You're being paranoid. We work together. We'll continue to argue, pout, shout, and do all the things we've been doing that people expect us to do. As long as we continue to turn out good work, no one will think we're an item. I won't be hanging out in your office, and you won't be hanging out in mine unless we are talking about an assignment. We won't be holding hands at your drawing board or hiding under my desk with a '*Don't Disturb*' sign hanging on my office door."

"Then why did you steal one from the inn? You took a 'Don't Disturb' sign from the last place we stayed."

"You saw that?"

"Yes I did!"

"Well, I thought you could hang it on your bedroom door when you walk around naked in there. It might keep me from thinking about invading your room ... privacy."

"Funny. You're trying to be funny. I'm serious, and I tell you this won't work!"

"We're going to make it work"

And it started out that way.

They didn't go to lunch together often, and when they did an account guy or other 'creatives' were with them. They didn't arrive at work at the same time or leave together. He did watch her. And she knew he was watching and she'd tingle when she caught him. But they didn't make any obvious overtures that could be construed that they meant anything to one another.

At home, they invested time in each other's well being, but never to the final act of intimacy. When they neared that plateau. Gwen always said, "Whoa, Taylor!" And he usually answered, "Yeah, whoa is me!" He gave in easily to physical urges. Gwen could relegate intimacy to a corner of her mind without desire overwhelming her.

Taylor couldn't get used to seeing Gwen walk around the house half dressed. Knew he'd never get used to it. She walked to the washer/dryer in bra and pants with a basket of washing shortly after coming back from the Hershey vacation. As the washer filled, she unhooked her bra, eased out of her pants and tossed them into the washer with the rest of the load. Then she casually walked back to her bedroom with her wicked walk and a smile on her face. Walked right past Taylor as he sat in the kitchen reading the Wall Street Journal. Taylor's mouth dropped open as he gaped at her, then waited until she dressed and said, "No more! No more of that unless you're ready for fun and games! I mean it. It ain't fair. Ain't. ain't. ain't! That's the most beautiful body I've ever seen, and you can't parade around like that and expect me to remain sane."

Gwen knew the effect her nakedness would have on him when she did it. Enjoyed his reaction. Liked seeing him suffer, knowing he wasn't suffering at all, just enjoying the fleeting moment.

There were times apart. They still did the

things they once did before Gwen moved in, but not as often. Taylor stayed out late with his buddies at times. Gwen still went out with friends, but not as often. They went to a few parties together, when the parties didn't include anyone with whom they worked. Taylor played softball with the agency team, in Grant Park, in the ad agency softball league. A lot of the unattached women in the agency watched the games, and everyone would go to Uno's pizza joint after the game for pizza and beer. If Gwen and Taylor wound up sitting next to one another, no one seemed to think anything about it. Life was good.

Thirteen

A few weeks after the Hershey presentation, Kobecki was notified that they didn't get the the business. It was a nice, friendly letter, but didn't give any details as to why another agency had been chosen. It amounted to: "Thank you for participating." Short, not sweet, and unsatisfying. Kobecki called the Hershey contact person and politely asked what it was that turned them off in the agency presentation. The answer was twofold. The agency that Hershey had selected had offices in major markets throughout the U.S., and Kobecki didn't. Then a number of Hershey people didn't believe that positioning their chocolate bar as a health food would work. Kobecki didn't argue, but thought the Hershey guys had missed the point.

Fourteen

It was two months after Gwen had moved in with Taylor when her euphoria evaporated and fear and anxiety gripped her being. She had left the agency at five, heading for home, and just outside the building she saw him. Phil. He was standing on the opposite side of the street watching her. He smiled, waved, and then disappeared into the passing crowd.

Gwen stood there, paralyzed for a moment, and then went rushing back into the agency. She found Taylor in his office, talking on the phone and he motioned to her to take a chair. Hanging up, he said, "What's up? You look sick."

"Phil was out there when I left the office. On the other side of the street. Standing there. Waiting. He waved and I almost threw up." Gwen said this wringing her hands, twisting in her seat as if she were being attacked by some invisible phantom.

"Damn! Well, I figured the psycho would show up, sooner or later. I'll just have to pay Mr. Phil Fraizzer a visit."

"No, Taylor no! I don't want you getting hurt! No!"

"Calm down, Gwen. I won't get hurt. It won't be me hurting, and I don't want Phil hanging around trying to scare you."

"I am scared. Let's get out of here and go home."

"Well, if he's out there waiting, it wouldn't be a good idea to just head home. He might follow. That's not a good option. Let's get something to eat. By the time we finish, it won't be so crowded, and we'll be able to spot him if he's on the street."

"I don't feel like eating."

"You can watch me. I'm hungry. Come on, you'll have to eat something, too."

Taylor whistled for a cab and they went to Hamburger Hamlet, off Rush Street and ate. They talked about Phil. Wondered if it was just a chance meeting, that he might have just wandered by when Gwen hit the street. Gwen didn't think so. As they waited for the waitress, Taylor said, "We could go to a judge and get a restraining order. Should be easy enough when we explain how he destroyed everything in your apartment."

"How could I prove anything like that, Taylor?

It would be my word against his. He's a lawyer and would make me appear looney. He knows the law. He told me the other lawyers in his firm come to him for opinions and advice on a variety of legal problems. He wasn't bragging. He told me about some of the things he was involved in and thought most of his peers were stupid and inept."

"You mean we have to wait until he tries something? Hurts you again. Not a chance. I don't like this one bit."

"How do you think I feel?"

They went home by taxi with Taylor looking out the back window, imagining that they were being folowed. But nothing was behind them when the cab turned the corner near the townhouse.

Gwen didn't sleep naked that night. She slept with Taylor in pants and one of his tee-shirts, as he held her close. She was frightened, but felt safe in Taylor's arms. He was awake for a long time, trying to figure out what he might do to solve the problem of Phil, the madman.

****

A week after seeing Phil outside the agency building, Gwen got on the elevator at 5:00 P.M. to head home. When the crowded elevator's door opened on the floor below, Phil was there. He had been waiting for her. He boarded the car, turned, and faced the closing doors. He was standing right next to her now. Gwen found it hard to breathe, and as the car went down, down, down, she choked out, "Phil what are you doing here? What do you want? Leave me alone!"

Phil answered, "Are you talking to me, Miss?" As he looked her way, he had a smile on his face and continued with, "I'm sorry, but I'm afraid you've mistaken me for someone else." When, the elevator reached the ground floor, the doors opened, and Phil walked swiftly away toward the street.

****

Gwen turned around, got back in the elevator and sought the safety of her office. Waited there. Called home every five minutes, but Taylor didn't answer. Taylor had been in a client meeting in Oak Brook, twenty miles west of Chicago. When he walked in the door at home, the phone was ringing, and he missed the call. As he changed clothes, the phone began to ring again.

"Hello."

"Taylor, he was here. In the building."

"What?"

"Phil! Phil was in our building! Got on the elevator I was on. Stood right next to me for all seventeen floors!" Gwen screamed.

Concerned and alarmed, Taylor said, "Where are you now?"

"In my office! I came back here after he went out into the street. I don't know what to do!" Gwen was crying now.

"Stay put. Stay where you are. I'm coming. Is

anyone in the office other than you?"

"Stanley the paste up boy is here ... he's working late."

"I'm leaving right now. Wait for me."

Taylor had never laid eyes on Phil, but he made up his mind that that was going to change and change fast. When his cab was a block away from the agency, he got out and walked. As he hurried along, he looked for a guy he had never met even though he wouldn't recognize him if he saw him. Taylor walked past the agency, crossed the street and ambled back, but didn't see anyone who looked suspicious. Then he went in, and up to Gwen's office.

"There isn't anyone standing around, lurking in the shadows out there, so I guess he's gone." Taylor said looking at Gwen who looked as though she was sick.

"Taylor, I never dreamed this guy would be such a nightmare. When he tore up everything I owned, I thought that would be the end of it. I'm frightened."

"Where does he live Gwen?"

"Why?"

"I'm going to talk to him."

"Are you crazy? What are you going to talk to him about? "

"Just tell me what he looks like, his address, and I'll have a *'friendly'* conversation with him. You can't go on wondering when and where he'll turn up next. It's easy to intimidate a woman. If he knows there's someone else in the picture that won't be intimidated, I think he'll have second thoughts about the stalking bit. At least that's the way I see it. Now, give me his address."

"No, Taylor!"

"Oh, yes! Give me his address!"

Fifteen

"Who's there?" Phil said from behind his apartment door.

"Bob Burns from the Ajax Collection Agency."

"What collection agency?"

"Ajax! The collection agency that's collecting the money you owe Miss Savage."

"I don't know any Miss Savage."

At that Taylor began pounding on the door and yelling, "Open up, come on open up!"

"You've got the wrong party. Beat it! I don't know what you're talking about!"

But, Taylor didn't stop. He kept on beating the door, harder and harder than before.

Phil became furious, anger clouding his judgement; he yanked open his door.

At that instant Phil's face met Taylor's fist, and he went flying to the floor. Phil's nose was broken, his glasses no longer on his face, and Taylor's knee was now resting on his chest.

"I'm only going to tell you this once. Stay away from Gwen Savage! Stop all contact! Do you understand?"

"Go to hell!"

"Well, if that's the way you want it..." Taylor spit the words out as he slapped Phil's face from right to left, left to right and back again saying, "Stay away from her, Phil, stay away!" He then cold-cocked Phil with short, swift, explosive right to Phil's jaw. Then Taylor went through Phil's pockets, found his wallet, and emptied it of $415.00. As he was about to leave, he saw Phil's glasses on the floor and crushed them under his heel. "So long Phil ... hope you got my message," Taylor barked as Phil was starting to recover on the floor.

****

Phil staggered to his feet with his nose broken, upper lip split, and a front tooth broken at the gum line. He searched and found a second pair of glasses and then took a cab to the Northwestern Memorial Hospital. He told the admitting woman, in the emergency room, that he had been mugged. She called the police. Phil gave them a vague story about being robbed as he was about to enter his apartment building. The thief took over $400.00. Phil couldn't describe his assailant,

other than he was over six feet. No distinguishing fea-
tures that he could remember. A doctor taped his nose,
put two stitches in his lip, gave him some aspirin, and
told him to see his dentist. And that was that. Phil knew
it was a friend of Gwen's that did this to him. He
knew he would find out who that friend was, and that
he would take care of that friend. Permanently. It would
take some time, of course, but he had nothing better to
occupy his time. He told himself he would be harass-
ing Gwen forever. Maybe not soon, but she hadn't seen
the last of him. Not by a long shot. He would take care
of the bastard that mauled him before he did anything
else. No one did this to Phil Fraizzer and got away with
it.

****

After his little get-together with Phil, Taylor
cabbed it to the Gas Light Club on Huron. He called
Gwen and said he would be home late and not to worry.
She wanted to know what happened, and he explained
he had asked Phil not to bother her anymore and
thought that Phil understood. That was all. Then he
went to the bar, found a couple of buddies there and
had a few drinks. It was after midnight when he got
home and checked on Gwen. She was sound asleep.

****

The next day, Phil called Gwen at work as he
sat at home nursing his wounds. He screamed into the

phone, "Who did this to me you bitch?"

Gwen hung up immediately and told the switchboard she didn't want any more phone calls. Then she flew to Taylor's office, slammed the door behind her and said, "What have you done Taylor? Phil called. Screaming. What have you done?"

Taylor looked up at her. Smiled. Took an envelope from his desk and said, "Hey, I just bounced him around a little. He gave me $415.00 to pay for the damage he caused. It was all the cash he had, and I didn't want a check. I was afraid he'd call the bank and stop payment. It's in the envelope. Told him if he didn't stop bothering you he'd be in deep trouble. That's all I did."

"Taylor ... you're ... you're positively ... positively nuts! He's not going to think twice about bothering me!" Gwen wasn't whispering when she said it, and she was right.

Sixteen

Phil did nothing to disturb Gwen for more than a month. As he healed, he wanted Gwen and her boyfriend to relax and forget about him because that would make what he had in mind a lot easier. During that month he found that Taylor was the guy he had to take care of. Phil found that Taylor lived near Lincoln Park in a three story town house. He found out that Taylor Lowe had money, drove a Buick station wagon, ran in Lincoln Park for exercise, worked out at a Bally Fitness Center, had memberships in the Gas Light Club and Playboy Club, enjoyed eating at the Whitehall Club on Delaware, enjoyed pizza at Uno's, and that he frequented a basement bar a few doors east of State Street on Huron. He found out that Taylor played softball with his advertising agency's team in Grant Park, and usually worked long hours, making frequent trips to various clients and suppliers. He also discovered that Taylor liked visiting art museums, and attending Cubs, Bears and Blackhawk games. Phil found out that Taylor had played hockey in college. Taylor was a jock. Then he found out that Gwen was living with Taylor. That irritated Phil more than anything.

The finding was done by an investigator that Phil's law firm used on occasion, a man who knew Phil and had worked for him in a number of legal matters. The man had photographs of Taylor, Gwen, Taylor's town house, his station wagon ... pictures of Taylor and Gwen running in Lincoln Park, of the two in the Gas Light Club, of them eating at the Hamburger Hamlet, and a few other places.

The investigator didn't know this was a personal job he was doing for Phil, and he was paid by the law firm. Phil arranged that by opening a bogus job, adding a few hours of work on a time sheet, and closing the job for billing. The bill went to a post office box and was paid using a check from a bank account that Phil had opened using a fictitious name. With the information in hand he started to develop a plan.

****

"Gwen, I'm going to go to the Cubs game with Monroe and two clients from Parker Electric this afternoon. Then we're going to the Playboy for dinner and I don't imagine I'll be home before eight or nine."

"That's okay, I'm going to ask Mildred from accounting to have lunch. I owe her. Then I'm coming home from work. Have laundry to do and ironing."

"Wait until I get home to do your laundry. I'll help you load the washer."

"Very funny. You've changed your mind about watching me work, huh! Well, I'll manage somehow without those eyes ravaging my body ... thank you anyway."

"My eyes don't ravage. They appreciate and humbly admire the many subtle contours, curves, hills, and valleys of the body the Good Lord provided to you."

"The Good Lord and hours, hours, hours on the exercise equipment, in steam rooms and doing all those pool laps. Is that account executive Monroe any good? He's been trying to hit on me at work and is about as funny as you are. He's not bad looking though. I might just let him take me out."

"Hey! He's ugly, got bad breath, he's overweight, and if you date him, I'll get him fired."

"Jealousy becomes you."

"I'm not jealous."

****

The day was a big waste of time and energy. Cubs lost to the Braves by a run ... 6 to 7. Monroe, clients, and Taylor arrived at the Playboy at 4:30 P.M. Then drank too much. The clients, Howard Konrad and Leo Borkowski, were not great people to be with for a day. They expected to be catered to, were obnoxious at times, and Taylor wanted out, but knew Monroe was dying to be gone, too. When they finished dinner, Konrad and Borkowski wanted to hit the Rush Street bars. After a couple of drinks in Tony's Cellar, Taylor was looped and said, "So long, gotta go!"

"Hey, Taylor what's the rush? It's only 9:00 P.M. We want to go to the Gas Light," said Howard Konrad.

"No way, Howard. Your boss, old man Parker called, and said to get you guys home early."

"Taylor ... old man Parker is on the west coast, and he's never talked to a soul at the agency in his life."

"Yeah, well ...I'm sorry, but I've got a big day tomorrow and have to get home."

"Tomorrow's Saturday, Taylor!" said Monroe, "What kind of 'big day' are you talking about?" Monroe didn't want to be alone with Howard and Leo anymore than Taylor did.

"My Dad's got a 7:30 A.M. tee time at Lake Forest Country Club, and I'm filling in for one of his buddies who can't play. I'm sloshed and have to get sober. Sorry guys, but I have to go. Have fun at the Gas Light," Taylor waved as he staggered out the door.

The cool night air felt good. With bleary eyes, and too much to eat and drink under his belt, Taylor decided to walk home. He felt he could sober up and walk off some of excesses of the night along the way. It was slow going. His head had started aching.

Seventeen

Phil had been parked around the corner from Taylor's townhouse, east of Cleveland, for three nights straight. He was aware that Taylor had a habit of working late on many nights. He knew that Taylor often went to the Ricarrdo's bar to have a few drinks on Fridays after work. He knew that Gwen and Taylor never went home together. When he planned his kill, he rented a car at O'Hare using a fake South Dakota driver's license. Then he sat and waited in the dark.

He knew that Taylor had to cross the intersection ahead on his way home. After three nights he thought he might have made a mistake. He had almost fallen asleep when he caught some movement in his rearview mirror. It was Lowe coming down the street.

Taylor walked passed Phil's car not more than fifteen feet away. As Taylor approached Cleveland Avenue, Phil started the car. It should have been easy. It would have been, if Phil had a normal driving capability, but he was a lousy driver.

He didn't own a car, his reflexes were slow, and his judgement cloudy in regard to speed and distance. As he put the Ford in drive and stepped on the gas, it leaped ahead, burning rubber. Phil was off balance as he squealed around the corner with Taylor not more than 25 yards away in the middle of the street. As Phil floored the gas peddle, Taylor turned with rubber screeching in his ears and had but a moment to get out of danger. It had happened so fast he was momentarily frozen in his tracks. All he saw was the letters 'F O R D' on a hood getting bigger and bigger as one microsecond expanded to the next.

Then without thinking he feinted right, then dove left, but not before the side of the swerving, car slapped his hip and sent him flying over the curb and into the the parkway. He went down hard, rolled, and ended up in a sitting position as he watched the wayward car side-swipe a parked pickup as it went zig-zagging down the street.

****

"Shit. The bastard faked me out. But, I hit him," Phil uttered out loud as he struggled to get the car under control once again. He knew he'd have to ditch the car. He had hit a parked truck, mangled the side of his rental, and didn't want to be in any position where he had to explain what happened to anyone. He headed back to O'Hare and fast. He took side streets mostly. He parked the car in the airport's economy lot and abandoned it.

"I'll have to figure some other way to kill the son-of-a-bitch because he's not down for good," Phil said to himself as he rode the shuttle bus back to the O'Hare terminal where he caught a taxi, and headed for home.

****

Taylor was dazed. His right hip hurt, his head ached. His pants and jacket were torn. He had scraped his knees, bruised an arm, and cut his left hand as he fell and rolled. He thought he'd been hit by a drunk. The car was out of control as it had weaved down the block and out of sight Although the hip was painful, Taylor could walk, and he limped home.

He called the police. "I'm a victim of a hit and run. The guy hit a parked pickup on the street, too. No, I didn't get a license number. It was a Ford. Late model. Fairlane, I think. Yeah, I'll wait."

It took about a half-hour before the police showed. Taylor had waited for them outside not wanting to wake Gwen. The police talked to him for about ten minutes, left a note on the parked pickup, and left.

Taylor then went back into the house, climbed the stairs, and headed straight for his bathroom. He shucked his torn clothes, ran a hot bath, and gingerly sunk into the tub. His hip and the scrapes, bumps and bruises ached, but he considered himself lucky that nothing was broken but some skin. The hot water eased the pain a bit, and he dozed off. He woke with a start about 4:00 AM. The bath water was now cold, and he turned on the shower to warm up again. His hip had a black and blue patch; he put some band-aids on the scraped knees and his cut hand, dressed, and then brewed some coffee.

"You're up early Taylor, what gives? What time did you get home?" Gwen said as she came into the breakfast area in a robe with hair in curlers.

"Hi. Got home around eleven, but not before being hit by a car at the corner."

"What?"

"Yeah, some drunk rounded the corner on two wheels and side-swiped me. Ruined my pants, and jacket when I fell after diving to get out of the way. My hip hurts, but that's about all. I was sloshed and not my usual agile self. The son-of-a-bitch didn't stop. Called the cops. End of story."

"Are you all right?"

"Yeah, I'm okay."

"I'm sorry ... are you sure you're okay?"

"Yes, yes ... I'm playing golf with my Dad so I have to go. What are you doing today?"

"Meeting someone for lunch at the London House. Didn't finish ironing."

"Who's the someone?"

"I don't have to tell you everything."

"Yeah. Well, have a good time. See you later."

****

Phil went back to the drawing board. Murder isn't an easy thing to plan, but he wasn't about to give up.

Two weeks after his "hit and run" incident, Taylor was knocked off an El platform into the path of an oncoming train. He landed on his feet, dove over the electric third-rail to the next track, leaped to his feet and vaulted the six feet to the floor of the opposite commuter platform. The El had missed him by a hair's breath as it screamed to a halt. Taylor knew the shove had been deliberate. A shoulder had rammed into the small of his back and bulldozed him off the platform. If he hadn't been agile, fit, and quick witted ... as well as fast on his feet, he would have been dead. "Why?" That was all he could think about.

The engineer of the train that barely missed him had left his cab and yelled across the platform,

"Are you okay? Why did you jump? Are you nuts?"

"No, I'm not nuts, I was shoved. Didn't you see it? See something?" Taylor shouted back.

"All I saw was you going down!"

Then there was no more talk as another train rumbled by Taylor and the confused commuters waiting beside him. A few moments later there was no one on the platform across from him or beside him when both trains glided down the rails in opposite directions.

"Why would anyone do such a thing? What the hell is going on?" Taylor thought as he went down the

steps of the El station. On the street, he abandoned the idea of riding the El, and hailed a cab.

Most Wednesdays after work, Taylor went home, changed clothes, and then took the El north to Evanston. There he would meet his Dad and Mom for dinner at the Hotel Orrington and get caught up with what was going on in their life. They would listen to his tales of agency doings.

Up to this point Taylor hadn't mentioned that Gwen Savage was a part of his life, and living with him. His Dad would be okay with it, he was sure, but knew his Mom wouldn't like the idea even though nothing much had happened not to like at the moment. She might give him a thumbs up for his taking "the poor girl" in when she arrived at his home in distress, but wouldn't understand why he had offered to share his living quarters with her. She knew he didn't need any rent money. Taylor didn't mention his near death encounter of the day. It worried him, but he didn't want his folks to worry.

Taylor had explained to Gwen what he did most Wednesday evenings and never asked her to come along. She didn't think anything of it because they weren't in any kind of a permanent relationship. She thought she'd be a "third wheel," out of place. She thought his parents must be nice because Taylor was nice. One of the nicest guys she had run across in some time. Oh, he had an ego but not an obnoxious, overbearing one. It was hard not to have one when everyone kept applauding what he delivered at the agency, clients included.

Arriving home again, Taylor clued Gwen into the El happening, "Can't believe anyone would deliberately shove a person off an El platform."

When she heard all the details, Gwen paled and said, "Taylor, it's Phil. It's Phil! He's nuts. He could do that. Who else could it be?"

"Are you serious? He doesn't know who I am. He only saw me one time and only for a second. The few seconds it took to cold cock him. No, I don't think so."

"It's Phil. I know it's Phil. He's got the resources needed to find anything out. He bragged about that one time when we were dating. He works with all kinds of private detectives on cases that his firm has. He knows ... who you are ... where we live ... he knows!"

"Well, if it is him, I'll have to pay him another visit."

"What good is that going to do? When you knock on his door, he might have a gun and shoot you. That isn't a good idea."

"You think I should just turn the other cheek and let him kill me, huh? No, I have to change this guy's mind."

"Maybe, if I move out, he won't bother you any more." Gwen said trying to figure out an alternative to the rock and a hard place she was experiencing.

"Sure, then he'll be bothering you and I won't be around to keep things under control. Bad idea. We aren't going to do that!"

Gwen didn't want Taylor hurt and knew Phil

was cunning enough to do it. However, she didn't know how to solve the problem.

****

So Taylor turned the tables.

The next day he left the office a half-hour early, took a cab to Phil's office building and waited. He waited on the opposite side of LaSalle Street. When Phil exited the building at five minutes after five, Taylor followed. There was a rage building in every step he took as he kept his eyes on the spectacled, blond-haired lawyer walking ahead of him. The Italian Village restaurant was Phil's destination, and with the deluge of human kind leaving work in the Chicago Loop at 5:00 P.M., it took him almost ten minutes to get there.

Taylor waited outside the restaurant for about five minutes before entering. He told the hostess that he was meeting someone who was already seated and moved past her without waiting. Phil was alone, sitting in a booth.

As Taylor sat down across from him, he said, "Hi Phil, how's it going?" There was no smile on Taylor's face. His lips were tight, eyes menacing, and body poised to pounce if Phil made any threatening gestures.

"What? Who the hell are you? What do want?" Phil spat as he tried to figure out what to do. He was nervous, and remembered the first time he had laid eyes on Taylor at the door of his apartment, when he wasn't in control of what was happening.

"You know who I am. I know you. I want you to understand I'm going to break every bone in your body if you try any more of your hit and run tactics. You got that? You come close to me one more time and you'll be the one suffering, you creep. You yellow-bellied creep!"

Phil then realized that Lowe wasn't going to do anything physical, and the corner of his mouth turned into a sneer as he said, "Yeah, I do know you. Taylor Lowe. Champion of the fair Miss Savage. And I hear you. With all these threats I'm going to have to protect myself. Being a big, muscled jock isn't going to help you stop a bullet. That would certainly be my pleasure, I assure you. Oh, are you getting any, Taylor? No don't answer, I don't want to know. But give Gwen my regards, will you. I'd appreciate that. Now beat it, I want to enjoy my dinner. Beat it, or I'll call for a cop."

"I'm going to say this one last time. I'm not kidding. Back off, or you won't like the consequences."

As Taylor started to leave, Phil raised his voice and said, "HEY! Hey folks ... I need witnesses ... this guy is threatening me!" Heads turned as an exclamation point punctuated Phil's sentence in a voice loud enough to be heard by everyone in the dining room.

With that Taylor lost his cool, grabbed the water pitcher off the table, and poured it over Phil's head. Then, he waited for a few moments, hoping Phil would try to retaliate. Phil just sat there with water dripping off his long blond hair and glasses ... seething inside, but he made no move to give Taylor cause to lay him low. So Taylor left.

Eighteen

It was almost Christmas. For six weeks, Phil had been studying how to plant dynamite in the engine compartment of a car and have it explode when the driver turned the key in the ignition. He had seen the result in movies many times over and figured it couldn't be too hard to do, and he was right. He envisioned how the scene would look: the blast, the thunderous noise, particles of the garage falling everywhere, the fire, and Taylor Lowe dead. Torn apart. Burning. Taylor Lowe, understanding that instant before death, that Phil had his revenge. Phil laughed out loud when he thought of Taylor and parts of his mangled body burning beyond recognition.

Phil went through the bomb making and placing process, step by step ... over and over ... again and again ... until he believed he could do the job blindfolded. He found a source for dynamite that didn't ask who he was, or what he planned on doing with it. Four sticks were now tucked away safely in a light carryon type of travel bag. He felt that Taylor Lowe's demise would be a fitting present to give Gwen Savage on Christmas Eve or Christmas morning.

On December 23rd, Phil put on black pants, a black turtle neck sweater, and donned a black pea coat, gloves, and running shoes. On his head he wore a navy knit cap. He carried a small automatic in his jacket, just in case Taylor showed up unexpectedly. He waited until 3:00 A.M before he broke into Taylor's garage.

Getting inside wasn't difficult. It only took him about five minutes. Actually four, and because Taylor had left his Buick unlocked, Phil didn't have any trouble getting under its hood. Then, with a small flashlight in his mouth for light, he proceeded to place the charge and wire the Buick. The night was cold. Below zero. After taking off his gloves, the cold started to numb his hands, but he knew what he was doing and worked fast. He figured that Taylor would be driving to his folks home alone on Christmas, or Christmas Eve. Alone because the private investigator reports gave no indication that Gwen had ever met Taylor's parents. It didn't matter to Phil if she was in the car with Taylor. With Taylor out of the way, he wouldn't have any trouble dealing with Gwen if she was alive after the bomb went off.

As he fiddled with the bomb, he was excited, and his thoughts wandered: *When it happens. I'll be around to watch. I'll be here to see it, see the garage blow and watch him die. Watch them die, if she's with him. The neighborhood will be out in force minutes after the explosion, and I'll blend in with the crowd.*

He was right.

Only it wasn't Taylor or Gwen who suffered the big bang.

It was Phil.

And parts of Phil were blending in with the neighborhood crowd as they came rushing out in the wee hours of the morning to glimpse the rack and ruin of Taylor's garage. The neighbors were pouring out into the alley before the fire trucks arrived.

Phil had done everything by the book, and when the smoke cleared, the fire was doused, the arson investigators could only guess what had happened. A crossed wire, static electricity ... a mistake had happened and set the explosion in motion and scattered someone, the Buick, garage, and alley concrete far and wide. Back-yard windows were broken all down the street, and the backs of more than a few town-homes were scarred and gouged by flying debris.

****

Taylor had no idea it was his garage that had blown when the blast awakened him. The whole house had been shaken. As he came awake, he could hear glass breaking and he ran into the hall, thinking the townhouse was about to collapse. Gwen was up, in the hall with a blanket wrapped around her.

"What's happening, Taylor?" She said in a high, shrill voice that hurt Taylor's ears. She was wide eyed, frightened, and shaking, as she clutched the blanket tightly around her.

"Damned if I know. Maybe it's an earth quake ... or a gas main blew. Windows in back are gone. Got to get dressed and see what this is all about." He went back in his room, dressed fast, and went down to the first floor two steps at a time with Gwen not far behind him. Through the back door, he saw what was left of his garage. The scene was unreal. Grotesque. His garage was in shambles. Burning. His car a twisted mess of red hot metal. About ten people had already called the fire department when Taylor picked up his phone and dialed for help.

****

As the fire fighters got the situation under control, it was obvious that someone was dead, that the someone was connected to what had happened. The initial blast that had taken a life might have been an accident, but the intent was no accident, and the evidence was everywhere. Talking to Taylor, an arson investigator at the scene asked, "You know anything about this, whose remains we're picking up?"

"I don't know for sure, but it might be some guy who thought I stole his girlfriend."

"Did you?"

"No. The creep beat her up when she told him

to get lost, and she came to me for help. We work at the same company. Anyway, that's who I think might have caused this. He's been trying to hurt me for months."

"Oh, how so?"

"Tried to run me down, pushed me off an El platform."

"You're kidding, right?"

"No! I reported the hit and run to the police ... it was in September. Went to a Cubs game that day ... a Friday, the Cubs lost to the Braves. Came home late and a guy hit me with his car as I crossed the street. I think it was him. Didn't know it was him at the time, but right now I'm pretty sure. The cops should have a record of it. The hit and run. Then a few weeks later someone pushed me off the El Platform at the Fullerton stop. I was able to get out of the way of a train ... not by much ... the motorman of the oncoming train tried to stop. I'd have had it if I hadn't landed right and leaped over the third rail. The engineer must have reported it to someone. You can check it out. It was him, I'm sure of it."

"Okay. What's his name? This guy that has a hard-on for you?"

"Phil Fraizzer ... that's F r a i z z e r," Taylor said, spelling the name.

"Where can I find him, if he isn't the one scattered around."

"He's a lawyer. Works for Fields, Farmer, and Green on LaSalle Street."

****

Soon after the garage blew, all the local radio and television stations sent crews to the site; the Tribune and Sun Times had reporters on the scene before the fire was out. The media wanted to talk to Taylor. Taylor was more concerned about Gwen, and before anyone could get him on camera, he had hustled Gwen back into the house.

"Gwen stay put. I have to talk to the reporters and you don't have to be involved in this."

"Taylor, Phil did this ... he's dead ... it could have been you," and she was shivering with fear as she talked.

"It's over Gwen," Taylor interrupted, "The nut is dead. I assume it's him, unless he hired someone to do this. Please calm down ... make some coffee ... I'll be back here as quickly as I can." He said this as he pulled her close, hugged her, and tried to put her mind at ease.

****

All the reporters wanted to know what had happened and why, and Taylor said he had no idea. Whether they believed him made no difference, he stuck to the story. The arson investigator had cautioned him to be silent because, at this point, no one really could say for sure what had caused the destruction and who was to blame. He told Taylor that he could be in real trouble if he blamed someone who had no connection with what had happened.

Radio and television aired the story before Gwen and Taylor got to work. Everyone wanted Taylor to recount what he knew and what it was like waking up to chaos in the middle of the night. Ralph Kobecki told everyone to go home and have a great Christmas, because no one was doing any work. They were all talking about what had happened in Taylor's back yard.

****

On that same Christmas Eve, back at police headquarters, the arson inspector talked to two homicide detectives about what Taylor had told him.

"Taylor Lowe, the guy who lives in the townhouse where the garage blew, thinks the guy in the garage is a Phil Fraizzer. He's not sure, but Fraizzer is the only one he can point to that might have a motive. I don't think we'll find any fingers for printing or teeth to take to a dentist, but we better check this out.

"Lowe claims that the guy tried to snuff him a couple of times before last night. Check for a 'hit and run' report made near the end of September. Lowe says he went to a Cub game that day... Cubs lost to the Braves 6 to 7. Lowe also claims the Fraizzer guy pushed him off the Fullerton El platform on a Wednesday a couple of weeks after the hit and run. Told me some motorman could verify that he managed to get over the 3rd rail as the train went by. The engineer was mad. That's what he says. Lowe must have a guardian angel on his back if its true.

"Let's see if we can find anything in Lowe's background that might point to him as the bad guy here. You know: If Fraizzer did try to knock him off, maybe Lowe thought this would be a good way to waste his enemy. Tie him to his car and light a long match after putting dynamite in his mouth. In the process he'd have a way to get new wheels from an insurance policy. He was driving a Buick station wagon. It was five years old. Lowe has money, doesn't look like a looney, but who knows?

"And get a warrant and check Fraizzer's apartment. If we find dynamite, it's all over. If not, we keep on looking for Fraizzer and keep looking at Lowe. He'd have a motive."

The detectives got a warrant for Phil's place on December 27th. They asked neighbors when they had seen Mr. Fraizzer last. Most didn't even know who he was and couldn't help. His apartment looked as if no one lived there. It was neat, and nothing was out of place. There wasn't much food in the refrigerator or the pantry. They found that he liked to eat at the Italian Village, when they found his check book. Most of his canceled checks other than rent and those for utility payments were made out to the place. The warrant escapade might have been a complete washout if they hadn't found a briefcase in a closet that contained a bank account quite different than the one found pre -

ously. It belonged to someone named Fred Fox. Payments had been made by Fox to the law firm that Fraizzer worked for. There was an oversize envelope in the briefcase that contained photographs of Taylor Lowe and Miss Savage in a number of social situations along with pages of reports of surveillance by a private investigator. None of the photos suggested that Lowe and Savage were any more than friends or business acquaintances.

After finding the PI photos and reports, the detectives went to the offices of Fields, Farmer and Green. It accomplished nothing other than to find out that Phil Fraizzer hadn't been at work for days and hadn't been in contact.

The next day they talked to the private investigator who had made the reports concerning Lowe and Savage. He confirmed that Fraizzer had given him the surveillance job and it was for a client named Fox. He was paid by Fields, Farmer, and Green. Fraizzer had told the private investigator that Fox had been engaged to Savage, and he wanted to learn why she had broken the engagement, and who she was seeing. End of story. The PI said he had read the news story about Lowe's garage and figured Fox must have been involved.

"Why didn't you come forward and let us in on this?" One of the detectives wanted to know.

"I wanted to talk to Fraizzer first. I do a lot of business with him. He hasn't been at work. Thought he was the one who told you to see me."

"What's your impression of the relationship of Lowe and Savage?"

"Ask FF&G for my report and pictures. I took a lot of pictures. The two seemed close, but nothing I found indicated that they are more than friends and work together. She's living with him so they might be shacking up, but I can't prove it. Never caught them kissing or holding hands. Check with Fraizzer. Maybe Fox did the garage."

As far as the detectives could learn, Fred Fox didn't exist. After talking to the private investigator, they then went to visit Ralph Kobecki at his agency.

After being ushered into Kobecki's office, Ralph looked at his visitors and said, "Is this about Lowe's garage blowing up? Give me a minute and I'll get him in here."

"No, that won't be necessary. We are investigating him and need some answers from you."

"What? Why? He didn't have anything to do with the blowing up of his garage."

"We hope you're right, but we have to check him out. Do you know that Miss Savage is living with Lowe?"

"What? Nonsense!"

"It's true. Take a look at these photographs."

Kobecki was dumbfounded. There were more than a dozen pictures of Taylor and Gwen together in places far away from the office. Running together in Lincoln Park. Riding bikes along the lake shore. Eating at Chez Paul. On the steps of Taylor's townhouse. On a sail boat in Lake Michigan. Kobecki was stunned.

"Look, I didn't know the two were living together, seeing each other, but to think that Taylor could do anything as outrageous as blow up his garage or kill someone is ridiculous. I've know him since he went to Northwestern. He's worked here six years. He couldn't be involved in this."

"Well, we have to make sure. We have evidence that Lowe poured a pitcher of water over a guy named Fraizzer, as he was eating at the Italian Village. Fraizzer might be the dead body we found in Lowe's garage. Lowe was heard making threatening statements to the guy. So we have to check him out."

"Why would he do something like that?"

"According to Lowe, Fraizzer tried to kill him a couple of times before Lowe's garage blew."

"I don't know anything about that either," Koebecki said. "This doesn't sound anything like the Taylor Lowe I know."

The detectives then asked Kobecki if he would call Lowe and Savage into his office.

When they arrived, they had to go over all the events that led to their current situation. This time in more detail and included how the situation developed with Gwen and Taylor living together. The detectives took notes and then left, but not before they let Taylor know that he was a suspect.

****

"Wow, Taylor, I have to say this is a surprise. You two are living together?" Kobecki asked bewildered.

"It's not the way it appears, Ralph. Gwen is

renting a room at my place because of the circumstances. She's paying room and board. No more, no
less. We work together. We've become friends, better
friends because of what happened, but that's all. You
just heard how this happened. That's all there is to it."

"Did you ... no you couldn't have hurt him. Did
he really try to kill you?"

"Yes, he did. And I busted his nose ... roughed
him up because he was stalking Gwen, but the cops
don't know that. I guess that's what set him on a
course to try to hurt me. I confronted him at the Italian Village, doused him with water, tried to get him off
my back."

"The cops know about that, told me," Kobecki
said. "Now most of the people in the office will be
wondering why the police wanted to talk to Gwen.
How are we going to handle this?"

"I'm going to have to leave." Gwen wasn't
smiling when she said it. "This is going to hurt Taylor
and the agency if I stay."

"Don't be an ass, Gwen," Taylor spouted. "So,
they'll find out you're renting a room. All the office
gossip will die by the end of a week. You don't have to
go anywhere."

"Taylor's right, Gwen. You lost your apartment.
Taylor had a room to rent. You work together and
everything is working out fine. End of story. I'll handle
it." Ralph Kobecki liked both of these young people
and didn't want to lose either one.

****

Taylor was right. The small talk and innuendo ended in about a week after Kobecki informed the staff about the detective visit. For Gwen the whole scenario was a downer, and she was depressed.

Nineteen

As the new year worked its way toward February, Taylor spent most of his free time designing a new garage. He thought about asking the city for a permit to put a bachelor pad above it. A place to crash for those rare occasions when a guy got soused after watching the Bears or Blackhawks with him and couldn't make it home. Now that Gwen was living with him, he didn't want company staying the night anymore.

He bought a new car. A Lincoln. He liked big cars and the Lincoln was comfortable, easy to drive and smooth. It floated nicely over the bumps and pot holes of Chicago streets. On the long hauls it was a pleasure to navigate. Most of his agency peers liked BMWs, Mercedes ... fast, flashy machines. Taylor never had followed fads or trends. He knew what he

liked and followed his own path when making deci-
sions.

It was one of the reasons he was so successful
as an agency creative director. He admired good, solid
creativity but never emulated or copied it. He thought
that was akin to stealing. So his clients got fresh ideas.
Solid ideas based on sound marketing judgement that
helped make sales. That kept clients happy and coming
back for more.

Kobecki knew that Taylor was the best creative
guy on staff. Every time the agency ran into a problem
with a client, Kobecki called on Taylor to help bail the
agency out of the jam. Taylor loved operating in trou-
bled waters, coming up with creative answers and strategy that solved problems. Kobecki wanted him to head
up the whole creative department, but Taylor refused.
He liked getting close to his assigned accounts and
making things happen. He didn't want to supervise; he
wanted to continue creating "good stuff" for his group
of client customers. The clients didn't want Taylor to
disappear either. They liked him both professionally
and personally.

He also wanted to be close to Gwen. His job
permitted that. They could go on photo shoots together,
travel together to client meetings, and have conferences
without any loose talk or people wondering what was
going on. Everything was just dandy as far as Taylor
was concerned and he wanted to keep it that way.

The agency's other creative directors were en-
vious of Taylor's campaign triumphs. What he came
up with time and time again, seemed so easy for him.

They struggled, and Taylor waltzed. They didn't realize that he didn't leave his work at the office; it went home with him. He thought about his creative load all the time. He wrote headlines everywhere ... in the shower ... in bed ... watching TV ... reading a book ... having his morning coffee. He was always thinking about a problem to be solved.

At times, Gwen would be talking to him at home for minutes before she realized that he was off in never-never land thinking about an ad, a strategy, or a solution for some client deadline. She'd yell at him. Rant. Rave. Get pissed off, but she admired his drive, knew he was the best and that no one could change his work ethic.

He told her. "All you have to do to be successful is deliver ten percent more than the hardest working guy or gal in the agency and you'll never lose. You wind up number one. If you have a problem and need help from your boss, present the problem and tell him you think there are a couple of ways to solve it. Then tell him what you think.   I'll bet ten to one, he'll go with one of your choices ... he may embellish it a bit ... but you'll have solved the problem with his blessing. He won't forget that you didn't make him do all the work. That's a boss's biggest problem, people who expect him to bail them out of situations they should be able to take care of. It's easy to say, '*what do I do now boss.*' You can't get ahead that way."

Twenty

Four months had trickled by since the New Year started. Things were back to normal, with the exception being Taylor's garage. The hole in the ground had been filled, but no construction work had started. Work-wise, things were in good shape for Taylor and Gwen. Clients were happy. They both had had raises. It was a busy time in the agency with a couple of new clients and new year budgets keeping heads and hands churning out creative answers to marketing needs. A lot of "after hours" hours were being spent pecking away at typewriter keys and sharpening pencils at the agency drawing boards.

The plans for Taylor's new garage were finished. The contract had been signed. The city wouldn't give Taylor permission to put living quarters above it, but Taylor was okay with the fact that he couldn't beat City Hall. Phil was still missing. No one could identify what little there was left of the person responsible for the bombing. At the end of April, the homicide detectives informed Taylor that the investigation was over. They couldn't prove that Fraizzer was the person who had died in the garage, but they thought he was the guy. He hadn't shown up anywhere.

"Does Fraizzer have any relatives?" Taylor wanted to know.

"Not any that we have been able to turn up. Companies usually have a record of who to call in case of an emergency, but he left that information blank on his law firm records. He was a loner, but not a guy who would disappear without letting someone in the firm know where he was going. That's what they told us. And you're off the hook, Mr. Lowe. We can't find anything of consequence that points to your involvement."

"Thanks for filling me in. I appreciate it," Taylor told the cops as they left. He was happy 'Fraizzer's Folly' was behind him, and he didn't have to worry about it anymore.

****

Since the garage had blown, Gwen and Taylor's relationship had become strained. Gwen found it hard to overcome the feeling that she was responsible for Taylor's close encounter with death and Phil's dying. She was depressed couldn't shake the ominous feelings of the night before Christmas Eve.

She had fallen in love with Taylor. Although she hadn't said the words to him, she loved him. Yet, at the moment she was put off when he tried to kiss or touch her and didn't know why. Something was wrong about it; it felt wrong. Taylor was Taylor and though he didn't understand what was going on in Gwen's head, he decided that patience was the virtue that had to be applied. He tried to talk to her about what was happening to their relationship, but she didn't want to talk about it.

"Come on Gwen, what have I done to turn you off?"

"It isn't anything you've done, it's me. I feel like I've been cursed."

"Hey, that's crazy talk."

"Maybe I am crazy. I don't want to talk about this Taylor. I'm sorry, but I really don't know what to say about how I'm feeling."

"Anything to do with ... you know ... your period?"

"Damn it, Taylor! Just stop it! Drop it! Cut it out!"

So the conversation dried up for the day, the next day and the next.

Gwen was also having a tougher time with her job. Layouts were taking longer to execute. The work was still top notch, but it was taking longer to get to the finish line.

Taylor decided that getting away from home and the office might be the remedy that was needed to fix things. He felt the hole in the ground that once was the garage was what might be spooking Gwen and a change of venue might restore a smile to Gwen's face. He missed her smile. It was Wednesday, and the creative work load was well under control so he broached the subject.

"Gwen, how would you like to go to the Wisconsin Dells, Door County or Mackinac Island?"

"What do you mean?"

"Well, there aren't any jobs pending for the next week, so I thought we could skip out for a few days and have some fun. See some new things. What do you say?"

"How far away is Mackinac Island?

"About 400 miles as the crow flies. It's a beautiful drive if we go along the Lake. I'd like to get some miles on the Lincoln and what better way to do it."

"How long would it take to get there?"

"Eight or nine hours. We could leave in the morning around 7:00 A.M and be there about 3:00 P.M. in the afternoon. The Grand Hotel is supposed to be a great place to stay. There are no cars on the island. You travel by horse and buggy, ride a bike, or take a hike. They have a pool. What do you say? Let's do it."

"Sounds like you've already booked us in. You haven't, have you?"

"No! No ... but I'd like to."

"Taylor, I do need a break. I'm depressed. Should be happy, but I'm just not and I'm making you unhappy, too. I'm truly sorry."

"Great! One room or two?"

"We can do the one room bit again, but two

beds, Taylor. I'm still not ready for fun and games. Do you understand that?"

"Sure. No problem. We'll go on Saturday. I'll book a room for three days. Then we can take our time coming home and maybe stop in the Dells for a day. How does that sound."

"Sounds okay. I'll have to buy a swim suit."

"Want me to do that for you?"

"No, Taylor. I can just imagine what you'd pick out. I'm not the bikini type."

"You've got the body for one!"

"No one would know that better than you. Thanks! I'll buy a suit myself."

****

On Saturday they were out the door by 7:30 A.M. It was a beautiful day in Chicago as they headed north. They went through Milwaukee, traveled along the lake, stopped for lunch in Manitowoc, then traveled through Green Bay, and along the water to Menomonee and Escanaba. About 180 miles later they were at the dock, ready for the ferry trip to the to the island.

The weather had turned brisk, chilly and the waves coughed up white caps as the ferry crossed the water to the island. The hotel had a buggy at the dock to meet them when they landed.

The old hotel was beautiful. Getting a little worn in places, but beautiful nonetheless. It had opened in 1887, its season ran from May to the end of October and its front porch was said to be the longest porch in the world. Taylor didn't know why anyone would doubt it. It was long. The hotel had only been open a few days for the season, and the pool hadn't been filled, as yet. That was a downer for Taylor, because Gwen had told him he'd like the swim suit she had picked out.

Dinner at the hotel required a dress for ladies, and a suit, complete with tie, for gentlemen. After dinner on the first night, Taylor wanted a few after dinner drinks; Gwen wanted to go to bed. That's what she did, as Taylor sat on the grand, Grand Hotel front porch and sipped cognac in the cool night air. He watched the beacon of the old Spectacle Reef Light House out in the lake waters and thought about how fortunate ... how blessed ...he was. Blessed with family, work, and having Gwen drop into his life.

Although he didn't care to think about Phil in any positive light, he had him to thank for Gwen's appearance at his door and in his life. As he drained the last of the liquid from his glass, he walked back into the hotel and to his room. Gwen was asleep.

The next day they took a carriage tour of the island. After lunch they rented bikes and rode for two hours. Then, they sat on the porch and read books. Gwen fell asleep about twenty minutes after they had gotten comfortable. They skipped the hotel dinner that night, walked into the town, and ate at the Carriage House. At dinner, it seemed that Gwen was getting out of her funk. She had two glasses of wine and was a bit tipsy by the time they headed back to the hotel.

"Taylor, you've been so good to me; I don't know how I'll ever repay you."

"There's nothing to repay. Your company is re-payment enough. I enjoy being around you, working with you ... holding you, touching you when you let me."

"Tell me about the best girlfriend you ever had."

"Well, she knocked on my door one rainy night, naked and..."

"Taylor! You know what I mean ... the best other girl in your life."

"Well, in high school a girl ... probably the best looking girl in the whole school ... sort of tossed herself at me. I was on the hockey team. Played baseball. I was a letter jock. We dated the whole senior year, went to the prom together. She was special. We would ride bikes everywhere. I didn't have a car and my Dad did-n't like the idea of me using his wheels for dating. The north shore is beautiful for riding bikes. We would ride along the lake, around the Northwestern campus, and once we rode our bikes all the way to the Chicago Loop. Then when we graduated, she went off to Stan-ford, I went to Northwestern and that ended that."

"Did you write her when she went to Stan-ford?"

"No."

"How come?"

"I don't know. She didn't write me, I didn't write her. I think we were too busy, and too involved with college. We were friends, but that was all there was to it."

"Did you see her again when school was out?"

"No. Saw one of her girlfriends, the girlfriend said she had gotten engaged."

"You took her word for it?"

"Sure, why would she lie."

"That was the best girl you were ever involved with? Did you, you know...?"

"No, Gwen, I didn't get in her pants, didn't pop her bra. I was in a youth group at church. Church was a serious time for me. God was serious for me. Then at Northwestern, I wandered away from Him. I'm a sinner many times over. I've been involved with a lot of women ... girls ... but never have been in any serious relationship. It's been fun and games. Thought you might be fun and games too, at first. Now, I don't want fun and games. Fun sure, but no games. And it's time for me to get back to the Lord before it's too late. I keep thinking about Phil. If he had succeeded, I wouldn't have been in any shape to meet the Lord."

"What do you mean?"

"I believe in God the Father, Maker of heaven and earth, and in Jesus Christ, His only begotten Son. I believe in the Holy Spirit, etcetera, etcetera. I believe. Haven't you accepted Christ in your life?"

"No. Taylor. The only time I've been in church is to attend weddings and funerals. I don't know what it means to accept Christ."

"We have to change that."

"You really believe in the Bible, in Christ?"

"Let me ask you something. I've heard you say nature is a wonderful thing. I've heard you talk about butterflies, birds, horses, flowers, trees. Do you believe that the earth, the universe, and everything in it just happened? How could it just happen? The universe is too complex to be a happenstance. God made it and everything in it. You. Me. Everything! The Bible tells how it happened. How Christ came into the world, lived, died, arose from the dead. He died a horrible death for you, me, everyone who believes. Matthew, Mark, Luke, John ... the Apostles walked with Him. Prayed with Him. Watched as He performed miracles. His miracles were reported by too many people to be a lie. They happened. The Bible is the world's best seller. It tells the complete story. Read it and there's nothing to doubt. You have to believe!"

"Whoa! I wish I hadn't asked."

"Whoa, yourself. I'm going to make it my job to convince you. We're going to start going to church. Why did you start this conversation? What do you want?"

"I just wanted to know what you were like when you were young. I've gotten more than I bargained for."

"What were you like?"

"I'm going to tell you, but not tonight." When she said this, Taylor was putting the key to their room in the door. Gwen went straight into the bathroom, showered and got ready for bed. By the time Taylor finished his bathroom chores, Gwen was asleep.

On the trip back to Chicago they talked about work, they talked about many things, but the conversation about Gwen's past didn't surface. Nor did any more words about Taylor's belief in God. Taylor was confused. He hadn't been thinking about his relationship with God. Since the evening on the island, he was not only thinking about God but praising and thanking Him that he was alive and well. Phil had tried to kill him three times, and he survived it all. Phil was dead. Gwen was the catalyst for the life he had been living for the past year. Almost a year. Was it the Lord that brought Gwen to his door? He was beginning to think that it was.

****

"Gwen get up!" Taylor yelled through the bedroom door.

There was an understandable groan that emanated from behind Gwen's door, and then ... "What? Why Taylor? It's Sunday! Go away!"

"We're going to church."

"Oh, no Taylor. You go. Go away! Let me sleep." Gwen said as she turned over.

"Hey! I don't ask much. Come on, humor me. We're going."

"No!"

"Listen, you've been depressed, down in the dumps and I want you to try a new and different antidote for making your life a happy one again. Come to church with me."

"No. Not today!"

Taylor went without her.

After much needling, he finally got her to say yes. It took three weeks.

****

Gwen listened to the sermon. Listened to the music, the choir. Listened to the hymns but didn't sing. The words of the sermon, and the hymns gave her something to think about. When church was over, a number of people were friendly, and wanted to chat. She wasn't sure that this was an answer to anything, but she told Taylor she would go again.

She went to church with him for seven consecutive weeks. Something was happening to her ... no lightening struck, no thunder roared, and none of God's saving grace had penetrated her soul as far as she could tell, but she got interested in reading the Bible. She didn't know where to begin, but the minister quoted chapter and verse a lot during his sermon, and it was coming from passages all over the Bible. She asked Taylor how to go about reading it.

"I'll get you a study book, Gwen. That way you can follow along with a structured lesson. It will be better that way. I think starting with the New Testament, is the way to go. We can start with John, and I'll study along with you."

Gwen was on her way. Taylor bought her a Bible, a study manual, and small gold cross necklace. It wasn't long before Taylor had to buy another study book.

Twenty-one

Taylor was looking forward to Friday. He and his three golfing buddies had put together a fun filled weekend at a Wisconsin resort in Lake Geneva ... about eighty miles from home. It included a round of golf early on Saturday and sailing with their girl friends in the afternoon, with dinner at the Playboy resort in the evening.

The four girls were to drive up together and meet the guys for lunch. His mind kept wandering, thinking about the weekend, but Ralph Kobecki didn't notice. The two sat in Taylor's office. They had been talking for sometime about a client meeting scheduled for Wednesday. Tomorrow. Talking about strategy, what was needed, and now it was getting close to noon. Ralph was talking when Taylor's phone rang. When he answered, the voice on the other end of the line said, "Taylor, please come home."

"It was Gwen and he answered, "Now?"

"Yes, now!"

"What's going on?"

"I need you!"

"I don't understand?"

"Taylor, are you listening? I need you! Now! Tell who's ever sitting in your office that something important has come up and come home." Taylor then heard the receiver on the other end of the line click, and Gwen was gone.

"Ralph, something has come up and I have to leave."

"Trouble?"

"No. I should be back after lunch. I think we have everything covered for tomorrow, unless you have something else in mind."

"No, we're on the same page. I'm meeting Len Iverson for lunch at the Whitehall. Then, I'm going home. I'll see you tomorrow. Can you be in the office by eight?"

"Sure, no problem."

Taylor then left the office. It was pouring, windy, and he was lucky to get a cab before getting soaked. It had rained all night and hadn't let up. He didn't know why Gwen hadn't come to work. Didn't know why she called. Thought maybe the basement had flooded or the roof was leaking, although she never went in the basement. Maybe the disposal had backed up. It did that now and then, but she wouldn't call him if that was the problem. Why didn't she tell him what the problem was. *"Come home, I need you! Now!"* Boy, that's a first, Taylor thought. As he hurried up to the door of the townhouse, through the downpour, he mumbled to himself, "Well, here we are. No lights? Maybe the electricity has shut down. We'll soon see."

Taylor put his key in the slot, turned it, and heard the lock open. He grabbed the door knob, gave a push and when the door opened, he got the surprise of his life.

Gwen was standing there.

Holding a lighted candle.

Hair coifed.

Eyes sparkling.

Lips red.

Smiling at him.

Wearing the sexiest negligée he had ever laid eyes on.

For a moment, the scene took Taylor's breath away. Recovering, he gasped, "What ... what are you doing?"

Gwen put a finger to her lips for silence, took him by the hand, and led him upstairs. The corridor was dark, except for the candle-light, and all the shades were drawn. In her bedroom candles were burning, soft music was playing, and there was perfume in the air. A bottle of champagne was sitting in a bucket next to the turned down bed. Two glasses were sitting on the night stand. Taylor was mesmerized, but confused. He couldn't take his eyes off her. Wanted her. When he started to make a move toward her, she said one word:

"Wait!"

She then took his jacket off and laid it on a chair. Took off his tie, shirt, undershirt, unbuckled his belt, and had him sit on the bed so that she could pull off his pants after removing his shoes and socks. In the process, he reached for her again and again she said...

"Wait!"

There was no doubt in Gwen's mind that Taylor was ready for what she had in mind. She could tell that he was aching to hold her, wanted to kiss her, touch her, and do a million things, but it wasn't what she wanted. Yet!

Gwen then backed away from him. Stood a few feet away in the candle light, and facing him, she pulled the tie at the top of the negligée and it dropped to the floor. As her body came free from the diaphanous material, and the candle's flickering light danced over the contours of her body, Taylor's eyes were filled with love, and overwhelming desire.

Taylor had seen Gwen naked, but she was always moving, never like this. Just standing there. Smiling. Watching him look at her. As he consumed every inch of her beautiful body with loving eyes, he made Gwen feel like a work of art. After what seemed like an hour to Taylor, but only a seconds had passed, Gwen walked slowly to the bed, put her hands around Taylor's neck, bent and kissed him. Then pushed Taylor down, joined him, and kissed him again.

When their mouths finally parted, she whispered, "I'm yours, Taylor."

That afternoon, evening and well into the night the kissing, touching, merging, and melding of bodies went on unfathomable new adventures that included mind and spirit. It turned out to be a "*getting to know you*" experience totally different from anything Gwen or Taylor had known before. The hours were wrapped in love, trust and respect for one another. When sleep arrived, it arrived about the same time to both of them. If nature hadn't called for relief, Taylor would have overslept and been late for his meeting. He was showered, shaved, dressed and ready to leave as Gwen came awake. He sat on the bed and kissed her. Then, his mouth opened to say something, and Gwen beat him to it.

"Please, Taylor, don't ask me why. I don't want to talk about why; just savor the moment, that's what I intend to do. Please."

"I've never ...."

"Taylor, don't! You've got a meeting. Go. I'm not going in today. I'm going to call in sick."

"You're sick?"

"No, I'm going to sprinkle your aftershave on me, hug your pillow, wish you hadn't deserted me, and languish in bed all day. Goodbye, Taylor."

Taylor didn't want to go. He didn't want to leave Gwen out of his sight, he wanted to experience more of what happened. But that wasn't in the cards. He had to attend today's meeting and knew that the meeting would end by having dinner with Ralph and clients. He had to go. Gwen teased him by putting on the negligée once again and walking him down to the door. There she gave him a kiss that seemed to sum up the wonderful togetherness they had found. It left him tingling.

****

When the door was shut, Gwen turned, and said, "God forgive me," as she went up the stairs.

****

Twenty-two

It turned out to be an awful day for Taylor. He was the focus of much of the meeting, but when the focus was elsewhere, his mind drifted back to Gwen. The wonderful night. He loved her. He was going to make her his ... forever. The thought flooded his mind, his being, and he couldn't wait to get home. When he finally did get home that day, he found a nightmare waiting.

Gwen was gone.

He couldn't believe it ... understand it. Didn't know what to do, where to look, or who to call. Gwen was gone. Everything that was Gwen, was gone. Everything. Her clothes. Every trace. Her bed was made. The house keys were on the bed in her bedroom, It was as if she never existed. There was no note. Nothing. Taylor was devastated.

Taylor had never been afraid of anything ... until this moment. From grammar school on, he had confronted every problem that crossed his path and then some. When a school yard bully started to harass a boy that couldn't defend himself, Taylor stepped in and faced the intimidator. Taylor was two years younger, smaller, but he fought as though possessed by demons. Blackened the bully's eyes, cut his lip and sent him into school crying. Taylor's nose was bloodied, and he needed two stitches to close a wound in his right eyebrow.

Both the bully and Taylor were sent home from school that day. In high school he went sky diving and didn't tell his parents. On his first jump the main chute didn't open, but he managed to get the reserve open in time to avoid disaster. Then he demanded the pilot take him up again, because he hadn't got his money's worth ... didn't get to enjoy the scenery as he fell.

When he played hockey, he played clean, but when an adversary didn't, he'd pursue the guy with vengeance. The scar on his cheek came when a guy hit him with his hockey stick. Both Taylor and the guy wound up in the penalty box.

Taylor felt he was in the penalty box once again, but this time he didn't know why, or how long it would last. He was frightened because there was no one to confront, and nowhere to turn for answers. He wasn't in control. He knew it was a deliberate happening on Gwen's part and couldn't figure out why, or what to do to find her.

As the days rolled by, he did everything he could think of ... talked to friends ... suppliers ... but no one knew what had happened to Gwen or could help him. He got nowhere in his search. She had gone to the accounting department and was paid before she left, but no one in the department had any idea where she had gone. They had asked for a forwarding address because they would be sending a 1040 at the end of the year, but Gwen told them she would send the address to them once she got settled. They had asked where "settled" would be, and she changed the subject.

As the weeks turned into months, Taylor became resigned to the fact that he would never see her again, and heart continued to ache.

Twenty-three

The Corcade account had Taylor hopping. He had a lot to do to get ready for the sales meeting in Pebble Beach. He had slides to prepare, charts to make, research to accomplish, and he wanted to run down some appropriate gags to interject into his talk. He wasn't a wonderful presenter, not glib or a mesmerizer. He wanted to be sharp as possible, because a room full of salesmen, and women, were a tough audience to talk to when it came to advertising support for sales.

Taylor believed that sales people thought each sale was personal, and advertising didn't do much one way or another. In addition to his planning and attention to details, Taylor couldn't get Gwen off his mind.

Why Seattle, Mt. Vernon, or wherever she happened to be in Washington? Why the abrupt disappearance? The questions kept nagging him, and were responsible for many sleepless nights.

****

The sales meeting was wonderful. The days full of sunshine among an atmosphere and surroundings that made a person wish the meeting would last a month instead of three days. The landscape, ocean, and surroundings were unlike anyplace Taylor had been. He had been blessed with vacation days and excursions to a number a beautiful places in his life. His parents had enjoyed spending time in many fabled resorts and had the means that made it possible, but they had never ventured to Pebble Beach. Taylor thought the facilities were special, the Pebble Beach and Spy Glass golf courses among the finest he had played. They certainly created stories and tales to be remembered for a life-time.

****

As the foursome sat on the patio drinking beer, adjacent to the eighteenth green, Drew Daniels said, "Can you believe this guy? Taylor hit the flag on seventeen, the ball went into the trap and he was in the sand for three shots ... took a seven on the par three! After hitting the flag."

All at the table laughed and Taylor responded

with, "Hey, Drew, it took you three shots to get on the green and you never saw sand on that hole. Then you three putted for a six, so I lost to you by a shot. You want to talk about what you did on eighteen?"

"Well, I'd have had a par on the hole if I hadn't put two shots in the ocean."

The laughter and stories continued as the drinks flowed on the last day of the meeting. Taylor's presentation went well, and he handled the questions without a gaff. He was feeling good. The sales people liked the HO train idea, and most said there was no need for a test run.They wanted the program implemented, as soon as possible.

During the meeting days, when Taylor was able to get away from his client for a few hours, he went to Carmel. No where he had ventured before had so many quality art shops. The town was a tourist trap like no other he had seen. He filled his eyes with sculpture, oils, and water colors as he moved up and down the shop filled streets. He wished that Gwen was at his side; she loved being surrounded by good art, and they had spent hours in the Art Institute and art shops along Michigan Avenue. He knew she would love this place. He also enjoyed the aquarium in Monterey and wandering around in the Cannery Row area with its unique atmosphere. He wondered if Steinbeck would recognize the place.

Taylor was forced to stay over the weekend after the sales meeting ended. It was one of the "perks" for a job well done. Corcade's president wanted to play golf and his marketing VP, Dirk and Taylor

were the honored guests of his choice. The foursome
played 36 holes on Saturday and 18 more on Sunday.

On Monday morning, Dirk rode with Taylor to
San Francisco to catch planes home. Dirk wanted Taylor to come back to Seattle as quickly as could be
arranged, because he wanted the advertising program
implemented. There were a number of important details that needed to be discussed and acted on.

****

On his next trip to Seattle, Taylor left a day
early for his Corcade meeting and rented a car at Sea-
Tac. Then, he drove directly to Mt. Vernon in plenty of
time to reach the Volkswagen dealership before it
closed. He explained to a salesman what he wanted and
the salesman turned Taylor over to the sales manager.

"That plate number isn't one we were involved
in getting," The man said, after he spent some time
checking. "The only red Karmann Ghia convertible we
ever sold was bought by an old geezer by the name of
Cunningham. He lives ... or did live ... on Toledo
Street in Bellingham. I tried his number, but it isn't in
service any longer. He may have a new number. One
thing's for sure, he hasn't had the car here for servicing
in over a year. He probably moved, but I have the address he had when he bought the car, if you'd like to
check it out."

Taylor left Mt. Vernon, drove to the Toledo
Street address in Bellingham and found it was a dead
end.

"Yes, Mr. Cunningham did live here. He sold the house to us and then moved to Vancouver," said the young woman that answered the door.

"Did he drive a red convertible?"

"No, As I remember, it was a black BMW sports car. Fancy. Fast. Expensive. That old Mr. Cunningham liked driving fast. I'd love to have a BMW or a convertible of any color, but we drive an old truck. My husband's a carpenter contractor."

Taylor thanked the woman, left, and then found a phone. He called information. He found there were eighty-five Cunninghams in Vancouver so he had to call the Mt. Vernon car dealer once again.

"Cuninngham's first name was Harold. He didn't like being called Harry. I remember that much. He's a crusty old tiger. Good luck."

Taylor then got three 'Harold Cunningham' phone numbers from information. The first two he tried weren't the right 'Harold.' When he tried the third number, no one answered, so Taylor left Bellingham and drove back to Seattle. It was about 8:00 P.M. when Harold number three finally answered his phone.

"Mr. Cunningham, my name is Taylor Lowe. I'm calling in an attempt to locate a friend. A friend that I believe may have bought your red Karmann Ghia some time ago. Did you live in Bellingham and own a Karmann Ghia?"

"How did you get my name, Mr. Lowe?"

"I found you through the Mt. Vernon, Volkswagen dealer."

"Why in the hell would they give you any information about me. What 'yah' want with me?"

"I'm sorry to bother you, Mr. Cunningham, but I'm trying to locate a friend, a woman, a woman that meant a lot to me, and I believe she bought that convertible you used to own."

"Don't know where yah got that idea. I sold that car to a man. An old guy. Younger than me, but not a youngster. I didn't like the Ghia. Looked good, but it was slow on the pickup. I sold it and bought a BMW. Now, this is one hot car. It really rolls, and it's a lot classier than the Ghia."

Taylor took a chance and interrupted, "Mr. Cunningham, was the man's name 'Savage' by any chance?"

"I'm not about to tell you what his name is, son. Don't like anyone nosing into my business or using a phone to pry into my life. Good-bye!"

Taylor looked at the phone in his hand, trying to figure out if he should call old Harold again, but decided not to. Using what seemed like his last alternative, Taylor called Mike Danna, the cop who drove the taxi. There was no answer. When he called again an hour later, Danna picked up and Taylor explained all that had happened.

"Give me the plate number again and I'll get back you." Danna told him.

As Taylor was leaving his room the next morning the phone rang.

"Hello."

"Taylor?"

"Yes."

"Hi, Mike Danna. That plate number you gave me is registered to a Ben Savage, and he lives on Whidbey Isand."

"Whidbey Island?"

"Yeah, Taylor. Whidbey's an island. Isn't tough to get to. There's a Ferry out of Mukilteo that will get you there. I think she's living on a farm ... here's the address ..."

Taylor thanked Officer Danna, and wondered if he really had found Gwen, and more than curious about what she was doing here.

****

Taylor left for Chicago the next morning because he had a number of client meetings scheduled. He didn't want to leave Seattle, but had no choice. His next trip to Washington was two weeks away. The time was tough to contemplate because he wanted Gwen 'right now.' There wasn't anything he could do about it except immerse himself in work.

Twenty-four

The Whidbey Island farm was on high ground, and Taylor could see Puget Sound in the distance. The barn needed a coat of paint, the old farm house was in good repair, and its paint appeared to be of recent vintage. The paint was white, the trim a bright inviting green. Taylor didn't know a thing about farms, but he thought this one looked to be in reasonably good shape. He parked, walked to the porch, and went up the three steps that led to the door. He looked for a bell. There was no bell. No knocker. So he balled his hand into a fist, and rapped on the door. Knocked a couple more times. And waited.

Gwen was working at her drawing board in her second floor studio-bedroom when she heard someone knocking. She got up from her drawing board and looked out the window. In the drive sat a car she didn't recognize, and hardly anyone that she didn't know ever arrived at the Savage Farm house. Probably, a lost soul or a salesman, she thought. Her uncle was off to Bellingham, and she knew he wouldn't be home for some time. So, she yelled out the window for the visitor to wait a minute, as she washed and dried her hands.

Taylor knew the voice. He'd found her. He wanted to break down the solid oak door in front of him, but had to wait.

When Gwen opened the door, the shock floored her. She took a couple of steps back, hit the first step of the staircase, and went down on her rump with her mouth open and unable to utter a word.

"Hi!" Taylor said.

Recovering, Gwen said, "Taylor! How did you find me? What are you doing here? How in the world did you get here?" Then she jumped to her feet and stood partly behind the door and closed it slightly.

"Well, it took some doing. Can I come in?"

"No ... Oh, Taylor. I never wanted to see you again. Didn't want this to happen," and then she started to sob.

"Hey. Please don't do that. What did I do? Why did you take off? Leave Chicago without a word? Why?"

As she regained her composure and without

looking at him, she motioned Taylor to come in. Then, she walked toward the kitchen with him close behind. Taylor thought she looked beautiful. The walk filled him with a million memories. She had on jeans, an old sweat shirt with paint spots ... an old one that had belonged to him ... and her feet were bare. She didn't have on any makeup. No lipstick. Nothing. Taylor thought she didn't need any. She'd done something to her hair. It was a young boy type of cut. So short you could see her scalp. She still looked beautiful to him, short hair and all.

The kitchen was small. The kitchen sink was against a wall, and Taylor could see Puget Sound through the window above it. That's where Gwen stood, leaning back against the sink. There was a table between them now, and to Taylor it seemed that Gwen didn't want him getting close to her.

"Taylor you really don't want to know why I left Chicago. I had to, and that's all you need to know." She was now able to talk again. She dried her eyes on her sleeve, looked at him, and she wasn't smiling. "It wasn't anything you did or didn't do. You ... me ... it was fun while it lasted, concentrate on that and forget about me."

"I can't do that. Don't you think you owe me some kind of explanation? I'm in love with you. Thought you loved me. I know you love me or that night before you left was an aberration. I know I didn't ask you to marry me, but I thought you knew that it was going to happen. Should have. I know I should have! Is that it? I thought we were good for each other.

I know we're good for each other! What's wrong? Phil's dead. He can't touch you, us. What happened to turn you off?" Taylor blew the words at her. Like ice.

Gwen could feel his frustration, but didn't say anything. She looked at him. The frown stayed on her mouth, her brown eyes cold and sad and distant. Then, she turned her head and looked out the window, contemplating, biting her lip, and trying to decide what to do. For Taylor, the silence was awful. Then, when Gwen heard Taylor stepping toward her around the table, she said, "Stop! Don't come near me Taylor. Stop!"

Taylor backed off. Bewildered. Stood looking at her, and said, "Why ... why are you doing this to me?"

As she faced him, she made up her mind. Looking him right in the eyes, her frown deepened and she grabbed the bottom of her sweat shirt and in one swift move pulled it off over her head.

Now it was Taylor's turn to register shock. He felt sick.

"Pretty, huh?" Gwen said, looking at him.

Gwen's left breast was gone. Scar tissue defaced the beautiful chest that Taylor had caressed, kissed and dreamed about, since Gwen had left him. She saw the horror in his eyes. Something she never wanted to see, and now the moment was here, and she felt she had been right when she made the decision to leave him.

"Now you know. There's nothing more to talk about," Gwen said as she pulled the sweat shirt over her head again, and turned away from him.

A cold shiver went down Taylor's back. He couldn't believe his eyes or what had happened. He was stunned, hurt, mad, sorry, bewildered ... emotionally a basket case.

When he finally found his voice, he said, "There's plenty to talk about. You left because you found out you had breast cancer? I'm a big boy. What did you think I'd do when I found out? You figured I'd fall out of love with you? You mean a hell of a lot more to me than a boob. I should have been there to help you with this. Don't you know that?"

"No, I don't Taylor. I'm not feeling sorry for myself. I'm missing a part of me that I wish wasn't missing. I've survived, but we won't know that for sure for another five years or so. I didn't and don't want to involve you in this."

Gwen was sobbing again and in a loud, shrieking voice, added, "We're through Taylor. Through! Go! The sooner you forget about me, the better! Please ... please go and leave me alone!"

"Wait just a minute. I'm not going to let you get away with this., or get away from me again. We can start over. I'm just a guy that knocked on your door and would like a date. I've got a Seattle account I work with, so I'll be around. I believe the Good Lord has answered my prayers and helped me find you. We've been apart for over a year and we have to get reacquainted. I'll go, because it's obvious you need some time to think about this, but I'll be back. I need you in my life."

"Get out of here!" Gwen screamed and she sat down on the kitchen floor, buried her head in her hands and continued sobbing.

"I'll go, but I'll be back. Count on it!" And a choked up Taylor went back to his car.

Taylor's sudden appearance flooded Gwen with what seemed like a million memories. Working with him. Developing the Hershey campaign, the fun trip to Amish country. Taylor's wit and corny sense of humor. That smile, the scar on his cheek, those eyes. His muscled body. His tenderness, caring, sharing, unselfishness. The laugh. All the fun they had had. She thought about the night before she left. Often! She daydreamed about it still. She remembered the horrors connected to Phil. How relieved she was when he died. She thought about the day she had found out about the breast cancer. She didn't believe it. The mammogram showed something. Then the something was biopsied, and it was cancer. She believed she had made the right decision to leave, and get the cancer taken care of in Seattle where her uncle could help her in recovery. Now, Taylor's showing up ... seeing him once again ... well, she wasn't so sure she had made the right move. But it was done. Over. She saw the horror in his eyes when he saw the result of surgery. *"I'm bitter, Tayor!"* Gwen thought to herself. *"I wish we had never met, because seeing you ... thinking about you ... hurts so much."*

Twenty-five

Taylor put the car in gear, but he didn't go far. He traveled down the farm road to the highway entrance. He stopped short of it, pulled over, and sat there trying to figure out what to do next. Gwen was so upset he had to leave, but he had to find a way to reason with her. Somehow convince her, prove to her, that his love for her mattered more than anything. He was sick. Telling himself he should have gone through this thing with her, should have been with her, and helped her. Why didn't she let him know what was going on? After she disappeared, the most memorable night of his existence felt like a dream. Unreal. But it wasn't fantasy. He wanted to relive what had happened, moment by moment, again and again. On this day, it wasn't likely to happen soon.

He sat in the car for some time. Thinking. Then not thinking. Fighting the urge to go back to the farm house. As he made up his mind to leave, a pickup truck turned into the road. It stopped, as it pulled along side of Taylor's car.

"You lost? Need help?" Said the man in the driver's seat.

"No. I know where I am. Are you Mr. Savage, Gwen's Dad?"

"No. I'm her Uncle Ben. Her Dad's dead. Who are you?"

"I'm Taylor Lowe. A guy she left hanging in Chicago over a year ago ... left without saying a word."

"Oh boy! You talked to her?"

"Yes."

"And?"

"She told me to get lost."

"She's had a rough time."

"I found that out about twenty minutes ago."

"She told you?"

"Not in so many words, but I figured it out."

"So what are you going to do?"

"Mr. Savage, I'd camp right here if I thought I could talk some sense into her. She's in shock after seeing me. I have to pull back a bit and try to figure out what to do next."

Then Gwen's uncle leaned through his window, thought a moment, and said, "Could we meet somewhere on Friday? I've got business I have to attend to tomorrow and Thursday. There's a place ... a restaurant ... where the Mukilteo ferry docks. Across from the lighthouse You know where that is?"

"Yes, I came that way."

"Meet me there on Friday. Around twleve ... or twelve-fifteen. The ferry is pretty punctual. Can you do that?"

"Whatever you say, if it will help me get Gwen back in my life."

"I'll try to help, but she's a stubborn woman. And call me Ben. Nobody calls me mister. And you're Taylor. See you Friday."

Then they went their separate ways.

Twenty-six

"Gwen! Gwen ... I'm home," her uncle said coming through the door.

Gwen didn't answer. The bathroom door was closed so Ben Savage went into the kitchen and went about making a pot of coffee. Then, he went through the mail he'd picked up. When he had disposed of everything but the bills, he got himself a cup of coffee and sat down at the kitchen table and opened the paper. Gwen didn't appear for a good twenty minutes. When she did, her eyes were red, nose runny, and she wasn't looking her normally radiant self.

"Something wrong? You sick?"

"No, just depressed. But I'm okay now. How's everything in Bellingham?"

"Got most of what I had to do done. Have to go back tomorrow and then up to Vancouver."

"Would you mind if I went with you?"

"No. I'd like that. You sure you're okay?"

"Yes, I'll be fine, not to worry!"

"Well, pack a bag. We'll be in Vancouver overnight."

****

Gwen's Uncle ... Ben Savage ... never married. He had inherited the family farm along with his brother, Gwen's Dad. Gwen was fourteen years old when her Mom and Dad were killed in an auto accident. Her uncle was Gwen's only living relative. Before the accident, Ben was a carouser. Enjoyed going to Seattle and Vancouver to drink and knock about. He was never the "life of the party," but liked watching those that were. More often than not, he'd wind up with a female who liked the strong, silent type ... he'd shack up for a couple of days and then head back to the farm.

He was rough cut, handsome with a weathered look, six feet tall, muscular, with brown hair, brown eyes, and always seemed to have a hint of a smile on his face. He had never found any woman who had turned his thoughts toward marriage. He had loved his brother. Loved his brother's wife. Loved his niece.

Then, he woke up one day and found his life changed. Overnight, he had become the mainstay in Gwen's life. Ben was only twenty-eight years old when it happened, five years younger than his brother. Most of the families, on Whidbey Island, who knew the Savages felt that Gwen should be placed in a foster home. Ben had asked her if that was what she wanted to do. The answer was an unequivocal, "No!" She wanted to stay on the farm. Ben moved back to the main house from his trailer home that sat next to the barn. He then changed his ways because he didn't want to set a bad example for Gwen to follow. It didn't do much good.

Gwen, the teenager, was already on a wild path. She didn't listen when he told her what she could and couldn't do. He wasn't her Dad or Mother; he was Uncle Ben. Ben! She never had called him Uncle Ben. And she didn't have to listen to him.

When fourteen turned into fifteen and sixteen was on the horizon, Ben found Gwen in his old trailer, stark naked with a stark naked boy. He had gone off to Seattle, became ill, and returned home sooner than expected to find the boy's bike leaning against the barn. Ben kicked the boy into the yard, threw his clothes after him and then turned Gwen over his knee and blistered her rear end. She had lost her virginity and Ben's trust on that fall afternoon. When the ranting, raving, howling and crying stopped, Gwen didn't talk to Ben for a month.

During that month the boy ... the love of Gwen's life ... started dating another girl. Then, she realized that all the heavy breathing and "I love you" talk the boy had done was done with one objective. She had been had, and that was it. That ended her play time with boys for more than a while.

She didn't date. She started doing what Ben asked her to do. She even apologized. Ben accepted, and told her what was done was done, and he wasn't going to judge her, but he didn't want her hurt or for her to put herself in harms way. He worried about her. Wasn't about to stop worrying about her. Gwen finally realized that Ben had given up his life to make sure she was safe and her life was under control. Something she could never repay along life's way.

****

They left for Bellingham at 7:30A.M. and Gwen and Ben didn't talk on the sixty odd miles from the farm to their destination. By 10:00 A.M., Ben was done in Bellingham and they were headed north up I-5 toward the border. Vancouver was another fifty miles away.

"Do you want to talk about it, Gwen?" Ben said when they were about ten miles north of Bellingham.

"What?"

"Come on, Gwen. Something's bothering you. I expect that Lowe showing up is what has done it."

Gwen abruptly turned her head toward her uncle.

"You saw Taylor?"

"He was parked near our mail box yesterday. I thought he was someone who had lost his way. The guy seemed nice."

"What did he say?"

"Only that you brushed him off. Again."

"He'll survive."

"Sounded to me like he doesn't want to survive without you."

"Ben, you know what I've got ahead of me. I'm through with the chemo, but no where near the finish line. The cancer can recur tomorrow. Next month. A year from now. Five years from now."

"Well, maybe he doesn't care."

"I care. Drop it, Ben. I don't want to talk about Taylor or what he thinks he wants. Did he tell you how he found me?"

"No."

"Well, let me enjoy the ride."

So they continued on without any small talk. No talk at all.

After Ben finished his business in Vancouver, he took Gwen on a tour of some of the places he liked to visit. Gastown, Stanley Park, and the Seawall Walk. They wound up at a bar and grill on Georgia Street. Ben had a Molson, and Gwen had a glass of white wine. They munched on some appetizers before calling it a night. Ben had booked two rooms in a hotel near Stanley Park, and in the morning they had breakfast before starting for home. A few miles south of the border Ben asked, "What kind of guy is Taylor?"

"I don't want to talk about Taylor."

"Come on Gwen. I'd just like to know your version of what the guy is like. You don't want to see him any more, so why not give me a clue. When you were living with him you told me he was a great guy."

"He is a great guy, Ben. I fell for him. Couldn't help myself. He'd die for me and almost did, but you know that story. He's smart. Has money. Should be looking for some nice girl to marry. End of story."

"I think he'd like to marry you."

"Yeah. He would, but that's not about to happen. He deserves better."

"I may have a bias, but there isn't a lot out there that is better than you. Give yourself a break. What if I'm not around to hold your hand if the cancer comes back. Then you've got nobody. It shouldn't be that way, especially when you love Taylor, and Taylor loves you."

"Ben, drop it"

****

Taylor had a table by a window that looked out into the Sound. He watched the Mukilteo ferry from his ring side seat. He watched it snuggle into the dock, watched the cars peel off. He saw Ben Savage come off the boat at a brisk pace as he walked toward the restaurant. When he came through the door, Taylor stood up, waved him over, and shook his hand. The hand was hard, calloused, and the grip firm. Taylor felt the grip was a good indication of what the man was like, and he wanted to like this man and for the man to like him.

"Hi, Ben. I prayed that you'd come."

"Said I would. I don't know how much good this is going to do, but hear me out. I was in Vancouver yesterday ... Gwen rode along. The only good thing to come out of the ride was that she admitted she's in love with you. Now, don't get excited. Hold on a minute. I'm happy she's in love with someone other than me, but she doesn't want to see you anymore. Emphatic about it, too."

"Damn."

"Taylor, I like you. Only because Gwen says she loves you. I don't know you from Adam. Your showing up here tells me that you might be the answer to what's been bothering me. She needs someone, someone aside from me. She's afraid, and I can't find a way to quell that fear. She's afraid that the cancer might come back and if she lets you back into her life, you'd be saddled with her. She can't live with that. They say that if she can get through five years without the cancer recurring, then it's a good bet that she's beaten it, but she doesn't want you mixed up in this. It's eating on her nerves. Robbing her of a good life. You have any idea what I'm talking about?"

"From my perspective that's bullshit. I want to be there for her everyday. I want to share the good, bad, and whatever life holds for her. I've got to figure some way to overcome her mind set. We've been apart for thirteen months. Ben, help me out here."

"Do you know what went on during those thirteen months?"

"Well, she had a mastectomy. That much I'm aware of."

"When she found out that she had cancer, she came home, and made arrangements to have the surgery done in Seattle. She was in the hospital less than a week. The healing took some time. Then she went through ten months of Chemo. And they were rough sessions. She'd be sick, vomit, and hurt. Lost all her hair. I was some comfort, I guess, but she was really down.

"While she was going through Chemo, she tried to get some freelance assignments from the businesses around Bellingham, Vancouver, Seattle, and Tacoma, but that's been rough going, too. She landed some work, and on a few assignments she couldn't deliver overnight and lost the business because of it. People don't have much tolerance for others these days, no matter what they are going through. So, she's bitter but hasn't given up. Got a question for you. How did you find us? Gwen said she never gave anyone our Whidbey address."

Taylor thought a minute before answering and then said, "I think it was Divine Providence."

"Come on, Taylor ... do you really believe that?"

"Didn't occur to me before ...but ... yes, I do."

"Explain that to me."

"Well, I assume you know how we came together in the first place. Then she disappeared. Over a year later, I get on a plane to Seattle, had coffee dumped on me while in the air. Then I have to find a new shirt and tie fast. So I go to Nordstrom and see her leaving the store. Lose her again before I can get to her. Miraculously, she turns up driving a red convertible in front of my cab. I tell the cab driver to follow, but I have an appointment and have to abandon the chase ... abandon it before finding out where Gwen was going. Then the cab driver gives me her plate number. He's a cop ... moonlighting ... uses the plate registration to help me find your address. I'm convinced God put me where I needed to be to find Gwen again. Gave me the direction and answers I needed to find you. It didn't just happen, couldn't have. I think the Lord wants Gwen and me to be together."

"I don't know much about Divine Providence. It is strange, I'll grant you that. I'm happy it happened. I'll be a lot happier if you two get together again. If that happens, maybe I'll start going to church!"

"Thanks for buying the red Ghia. If she hadn't been driving it with the top down, I'd never have spotted her."

"Bought it to help cheer her up. She needed wheels to make business calls."

"I had a phone conversation with the guy you bought it from ... Mr. Cunningham."

"You talked to Harold?"

"He wasn't any help. Told me to get lost ... words to that effect."

"He's a tough old SOB. We went back and forth for a month over the price he was asking for the Ghia. I finally gave up and wrote a check."

"Ben, I have an idea. If I can pull it off, Gwen and I might be working together again. If that happens, I think I'd have a good chance of getting her back."

"Great! I raised that kid from fourteen on, and I'd like to see her happy again. So pull off your miracle. Now, I have to get going. I have to get that ferry before it takes off. I assume we'll be hearing from you somewhere along the line."

"One way or another, you can bet on it. Thought we were having lunch."

"Some other time. Have you ever had steamed clams?"

"No."

"Try 'em, you'll like 'em. They're good here. See yah."

"Wait a minute. Give me your phone number. I need a way to get in touch with you."

Ben pulled out his wallet, pulled out a card, and gave it to Taylor.

"Never had a business card until Gwen came home. Thought I needed to look like something. The card makes me look like General Motors. You can reach me at that number. Gwen doesn't answer my phone."

"Good! Thanks."

Ben was practically out the door and moving fast before the 'thanks' left Taylor's mouth. Taylor watched the ferry head toward Whidbey Island, ordered steamed clams, and as he had been told, he found they were delicious.

Twenty-seven

Taylor did some planning as he drove back to his Seattle hotel. When he got there, he called Drew Daniels. Drew and he had become friends, in addition to the client-agency working relationship they had. They respected each other's opinions and were achieving some good results with the campaigns in place and moving forward.

"Drew? Taylor here."

"Hi ... when you left the office this morning you told me you had something going on this evening. What's up? Didn't think I'd hear from you again this trip."

"Well, I finished what I set out to do, and I'm free for dinner if you're available."

"What did you have in mind?"

"You pick the spot. Something reasonably quiet. About six or so."

"I'll get back to you."

"Thanks Drew."

****

Taylor met Drew at a cafe on Pike Street. Drew knew the owner, and they had a reasonably quiet booth. After a couple of drinks and appetizers, Taylor said, "Drew, I've been meaning to talk to you about something. Didn't know how to bring it up, until you told me that Harry was retiring when we were at Pebble Beach."

Harry Mandel had been Corcade's ad manager before Drew was given the job. Dirk Davis told Drew that Harry was to be in charge of print promotion material, catalogs, and the like until he retired. Drew and Harry had been working together for about a year, and now Harry would be gone from Corcade within a week's time. Drew was in charge of Harry's going away party.

Drew said, "You want to talk about Harry? Harry's a good old guy. He and Davis go way back. He's moving to Southern California. Has a daughter that lives near San Diego. What about him?"

"It's not about him, it's about the collateral material he's been producing. I don't know if you plan to replace him, but I think the printed material you have needs help."

"What kind of help?"

"Graphics and design help. There's no continuity. No consistency. The pieces are written well, but there's no family resemblance."

"You're right about that. Harry's a good writer, but he surrounded himself with a number of freelance designers, and that's why everything is so different."

"Well, when he's gone I'd ..."

Drew interrupted, "No, Taylor. We can't afford the agency prices for catalog work. Sorry about that, but that's the way it is."

"I'm not suggesting we take over the catalog work, but you need a solid source for design, and I know someone that's local that has great design capabilities. She would be able to provide a new look that would make everything cohesive and work together. Your logo needs some tweaking, too, and Gwen would provide the type of design answers that you would appreciate."

"Gwen?"

"Yes, Gwen Savage. She used to be the number one designer on my creative team. She left the agency more than a year ago because she had breast cancer. She lives on Whidbey Island."

"Well, give me her number ..."

"No. Can't do that just now. I'll tell you what's behind this, and I hope you'll understand what I'm trying to do."

Taylor then confided in Drew, told him the whole story of his relationship with Gwen and how he found her once again, and why that relationship was so sensitive at the moment.

"Okay. I don't have any print work at the moment, and I like your idea about giving all our printed material a family resemblance. I know that's been lacking, and now is the time to do something about it. Is this going to cost me an arm and leg?"

"I don't know what she charges, but this is a big project, and I'm sure you'll be able to negotiate a good price. You'll like her, her work, and it's going to help her feel good about herself once again. That is going to help me."

"I trust you Taylor. How am I going to get together with her?"

"I'll think of something and get back to you, okay."

"Sure. Gwen Savage. I look forward to meeting her."

****

Taylor called Ben's number a couple of times before he left for Chicago, but got no answer.   As he settled in his seat for the flight home, Taylor thought, *In order for this to work, I need Ben's help.*

****

"Ben? Taylor!"

"Hi. Was wondering when you'd call."

"Well, I tried before I came back to Chicago, but got no answer. Doesn't matter. I've got an idea, and in a couple of days I'll let you know how you can help me. Will you be home?"

"Yah, I'm not going anywhere in the next two weeks."

****

Taylor then talked to Kobecki and said he was taking vacation time at the end of the week, and would be the gone for a couple of weeks.

"Sort of sudden, isn't it, Taylor?"

"Yes, it is Ralph, but I have most of my assignments completed, and they all will be done by the end of week. Corcade gave me a trade-show promotion assignment before I left Seattle, and I did most of the work for it on the plane coming home. Layouts, and all that's required, will be finished by Friday. On Monday, I'll deliver the package to Corcade and take my vacation starting from there."

"You like Seattle, don't you?"

"I like the whole Pacific Northwest ... the mountains, Puget Sound, Indian lore, great golf, and beauty everywhere you look. On a good day you can spot whales in the Sound. In the fall, salmon head upstream from the Sound to lay eggs, and start a new life cycle. In the spring, acres and acres of tulips, daffodils, lilies, and irises bloom. They say the colors are spectacular. I've never been anywhere quite like it."

"Rains a lot, doesn't it?"

"Yeah, it rains, and it's the reason everything is so lush, and green, and the air is fresh and clean. It's a wonderful place."

"Keep talking, Taylor. I'm going to get in touch with the Washington tourism office and have you pitch the account. Sounds like you are ready to make a presentation."

"Ralph, there's another reason I like it. I've found Gwen again."

"No! How did that happen? Did she call you?"

"No, found her by accident." Then Taylor filled Ralph in on the details.

"Do you think she'll come around and see that you're sincere. That you want to help her?"

"I'm praying she will, and I'm going to do everything I can to convince her."

"Well, good luck, and make sure you get your time sheets in before you take off."

Then Taylor called Drew and Ben and outlined what he would like to do.

****

"Gwen, I've got a job possibility for you."

"Oh? You're my rep now, Ben?"

"I was in Seattle and ran into an old drinking buddy. He works for Corcade Paper. Did work for Corcade, he just retired. He was their ad manager ... in charge of printing material, something like that. He said the guy that replaced him is looking for design help, layouts, stuff like that. I asked him the guy's name. It's Drew Daniels. You should give him a call."

Gwen did.

****

"Mr. Daniels?"

"Yes?"

"My name is Gwen Savage, and I understand you might need some design help. I'd like an interview."

"What's your background?"

"I've worked for Ward's and two Chicago ad agencies. Just recently moved back here and I'm trying to establish my own design studio. I've got some terrific samples of what I've done, and I'd like to show them to you."

"Okay. Let me check my calender. Can I call you back?"

"Sure, my number here is...."

****

"She called, Taylor. Wants an interview. Told her I'd get back to her."

****

On the day of the interview Gwen was up at daybreak. She showered, dressed very carefully in a simple sundress, and she wore a cute mariner cap to hide her close cropped hair. Around her neck she put on the gold cross that Taylor had given her, the one she had held tightly in her hands as she prayed before having surgery. She had accepted Christ. Having His love had helped during recovery and helped comfort her as she went though the grueling hours of chemotherapy. She had to admit that she had missed Taylor ... missed his loving arms, and kisses, missed his being with her at the hospital, and through the long healing process.

As she ate her breakfast and drank her coffee, she thought of Taylor. The time they had been together. She remembered the day before she left Chicago. His overwhelming love for her. She had left that behind when she found she had cancer. She turned him away when he found her again. Now she felt regret having done so.

On the drive to the Mukilteo Ferry and on to Seattle she put her thoughts of Taylor away and concentrated on what she was going to say to Mr. Daniels. She had good things to show him. Most were things she had done with Taylor. She wanted to impress Daniels and prayed all the way to the Corcade offices.

****

"Your samples are great, Miss Savage. I think we can work something out. I had someone in-house doing the writing of our catalogs, but I'm turning the writing over to my ad agency. They charge way too much for layout and design work so that's why I need someone. Your hourly cost seems to work for me ... you say you're pretty quick, so I'm going to give you an assignment.

"We have four divisions. We need a corporate identity guide that brings all four divisions under a design umbrella ... provides a cohesive look for all our divisional printed materials. Once the guide is approved, we'll be revamping all of our catalogs. I asked the agency to send our writer over. You'll have to work with him on the identity project. He's in the conference room down the hall. A good guy. But, if you two can't see eye-to-eye, we'll have to do something else. Why don't you go down to the conference room and introduce yourself. I'll be along in a minute."

Gwen walked down to the conference room with her sample case. She hoped and prayed that the copy guy would be a good guy to work with. The door was open, but there wasn't anyone in the room. She walked in and was about to take a seat, when she saw it. On the conference room table was a box of Crayolas.

Her heart skipped a beat. Crayolas! It could only mean one thing! Then, a familiar voice behind her said, "Open the box Gwen, please, open the box!"

She didn't turn. Knew it was Taylor standing behind her. Her eyes started to well up as she opened the box and found a beautiful diamond ring inside.

"Know you don't use crayons. Tossed 'em. But, I thought it was a nice looking box for what I have in mind. That ring in your hand says it all! I've come to Seattle to stay until you consent to wear it and the one that goes with it. I won't back down."

As a tear slipped down her cheek, she smiled and said, "You're asking me for a date?"

"Yes, a date for a wedding .... a honeymoon ... and a life ever after."

****

...

Cary Grant
&
Millie

What are the odds
of a young woman
losing three husbands
in a span of less than 5 years?

Far more than winning the Lottery!

Though she hadn't married for money,
Millie wound up with more green
than found in one of our National Forests.

And Cary Grant
isn't interested in her money!

...

Cary Grant and Millie

My name is Cary.

Cary Grant.

Yeah, Cary Grant.

My mother was enamored with the guy and since our surname is Grant, she had me baptized Cary. I'd say don't laugh, but it probably wouldn't do any good. A vast number of people standing in front of me have laughed, smiled, or choked trying not to laugh, after learning the name. And I've heard so many stifled giggles, coughs, and "what's that again" in phone conversations, I've long ago given up worrying about it. The name does have some advantages.

I'm a salesman and once introduced, no one forgets my name. I'd be hard to forget if my name was Archibald Alexander Leach. I'm 32, 6'2", 210 pounds, black hair and brown eyes, dark complexion and have a scar that runs from my hairline, down the left side of my forehead, through the cheek, winding up at the corner of my mouth. The result of an accident long ago. It left me with, what most consider, a wicked smile. Overall, I look pretty good. Not pretty, but not ugly, either.

I've been selling since I graduated from Stanford twelve years ago. I sell for Hybrid Semiconductor International or as most call the company: HSI. I travel the globe, have an expense account that enables me to bank or invest most of my commission money and I like it that way. I was married, but my ex-wife found another love, one that doesn't travel forever, and now she's happy, raising a family. Not mine.

Today was one of those heavy hitter days. Made a presentation this morning to Kom-X-Computer Corp at their Silicon Valley Headquarters, made a sale that will keep me in the high tax bracket for the year. Then we -- their marketing V.P., top engineer and a purchasing guy -- went to lunch. I had hired a limo. The waiting stretch drove us to San Francisco and an incredibly expensive restaurant on Fisherman's Wharf. The four course meal, with Golden Osetra Caviar and dessert was only $620.00. The six bottles of wine we consumed, another $2,375.00, for a not so grand total of $2,995.00. Excessive. You're thinking, '*excessive*' and you are perfectly right, but I had a contract signed and sealed in my pocket for over $7 million dollars of product, so taking these guys to a hamburger joint didn't seem an appropriate venue.

After waving good-bye to my good clients, as the limo again headed southwest into the setting sun, I went back inside the restaurant, bought a bottle of white burgundy. With my own credit card. A bargain at $550.00 bucks. Then I walked, staggered really, down along the wharf until I found a place to squat on a walkway along the bay. I didn't need another glass of wine. Wasn't going to drink one.

This bottle was a gift. For my ex-sister-in-law. Forgot to buy her a birthday card, so in my muddled mind, a bottle of wine and a toast to her good health seemed more appropriate. She's a woman of expensive tastes. So a bottle of anything cheap wouldn't do. The white burgundy in my paper sack is one of her favorites. As I poked her saved cell number into my I-Phone, I hoped she would be at home, in her condo on Nob Hill. As the phone connected, a mental picture of her came slowly into my mind's view.

My ex-sister-in-law is two years older than yours truly. At 34 she's extremely attractive, rich, highly opinionated about everything. She's into politics, fashion, sports, exercise ... the kind requiring physical effort, to sustain and improve her figure and fitness. Millicent Anderson-Baxter-Edmonds-Landon ... Millie to friends. These days I call her by her initials: Mabel. She doesn't like the nickname or me. Why she doesn't like me is a mystery that I would dearly love to solve.

Millie is a tall, vivacious blonde with blue eyes, a great shape, and legs that most women would die for. By the numbers, she's a 34-23-32. Stands 5'9" tall without heels ... but she's always in heels. She's got a glamourous face and smile. She's the kind of woman that makes heads turn whenever she enters a room or walks down the street.

The "Anderson" in her background is Scandinavian. Her Mom and Dad are second generation "Swedes." Anders Anderson, her Dad, owns and operates an upscale book store, in Rochester, Minnesota.

Millie met her first husband, Dr. James Baxter, in the mystery aisle of her Dad's book store. She was bending over, straightening out some misaligned books. When she looked up, there he was. In just a few moments, the good doctor wound up overwhelmed with her beauty and almost asked her to marry him then and there. He was on a consulting mission at Mayo clinic. Before his three week teaching assignment ended, he wined, dined, and totally captivated Millie, and she didn't hesitate when he popped the question. She was 24, Baxter 35. He lived and practiced in San

Francisco.

They had only been married 14 months when he died. They were on a ski trip in Aspen, when he made a wrong turn on the slopes and hit a tree going ... some think ... about seventy-five miles an hour. Millie lost a husband, but wound up with close to three-quarters of a million dollars after the funeral, taxes, and a trip to Hawaii, to help overcome her grief.

She met husband number two, Leon Edmonds, on a Maui sunrise, downhill, bike ride from the top of the Haleakala volcanic crater. She had had dinner with friends that lived on Kapalua Bay, with a marvelous view of the ocean. She had stayed longer than intended, and when walking through the lobby of her hotel, on her return, she picked up a folder on a bike ride. She liked what she read, talked to the concierge and never went to bed.

At 2:00AM she was whisked away from the hotel to the top of the volcano. When the sun came up with a kaleidoscope of amazing color, she found a tall, dark, good looking guy standing beside her. He needed a shave, but smelled good. Had on jeans and a sweat shirt, and wore a dynamite smile as he introduced himself as Lee Edmonds. Small talk came easy for both. Then down the mountain they went without a word, because you don't talk while traveling twenty-five miles down the mountain; around the back and fourth of curves and curves and more curves along the way.

When the trip ended, Lee asked for a date. Millie said no, told him that she had just lost her husband, but she gave him her cell phone number.

This led to a few months of phone conversations off and on. Then when Lee traveled to San Francisco -- about seven months after they met -- they had their first date. And then a second date. Three days after the second they set a date. Lee and Millie were married eleven months after the good Dr. Jim Baxter was planted in the ground.

Millie and Lee went back to Hawaii on their honeymoon. He insisted. He wanted to revisit the place they had first met. Four days after landing on Maui they went back up to the top of the volcano for another bike ride. Alas, on the trip down, Lee lost control of his bike. On a curve, he zipped off the road and flew three hundred feet down a cliff to his death. Since the day of his death was the first day the enamored couple had left the honeymoon suite, many thought that Lee might have been groggy from the lack of sleep. Since Lee had no close relatives, Millie had him cremated and his ashes scattered in the Pacific.

Lee was 48, a partner in a foreign car dealership located in Milwaukee. Millie received one million five for Lee's share in the firm. She sold his beautiful home in Cedarburg, twenty miles north of Milwaukee for another half million, but kept his condo on Green Bay in Door County, because she thought it might be a good investment.

A few weeks after losing Lee, Millie boarded the Queen Mary 2 and sailed to Southampton. The seven day cruise was elegant in every detail, but she was morose, unhappy and stayed in her Princess suite for most of the trip. After docking, she took a train to London and stayed in an old hotel near Hyde Park, and the Royal Albert Hall.

Seeing the sights of London for the fist time took some of sting out of widowhood. Millie, being an extremely curious person, found the city to be an endless array of sights and scenes that she couldn't get enough of. What she had imagined might be a brief stopover, turned into more than a month of slow methodical exploration; and finally led to the purchase of a two bedroom residence on Park Street; a Mayfair location close to the hotel where she had been staying. She hadn't intended to buy real estate, but she had money, loved London and that was that.

On a brief holiday in Switzerland, she met her third husband, John Landon. He was the president of a brokerage firm based in New York City. Another handsome guy who loved travel, was sixty years old, and had a personality and demeanor something like the Hollywood Cary Grant. Everybody loved John Landon, because he was the epitome of elegance, and good taste, and never let anyone pickup a check. He too bit the dust. After two years of marital bliss he had a heart attack and died while hosting a small dinner party at an ultra exclusive eatery in Greenwich Village. The paramedics arrived in four minutes after being called, but nothing they could do helped John from expiring, then and there.

Millie was devastated, and a multimillionaire. She had a checkbook, one credit card, owned property in London ... San Francisco... New York ... Bend, Oregon ... Carmel ... and in Door County, Wisconsin.

What are the odds of a young woman losing three husbands in a span of less than 5 years? Far more than winning the Lottery! And though she hadn't married for money, Millie wound up with more green than found in one of our National Forests.

****

My call to Millie went unanswered. I had called her private cell. Then I buzzed her answering service, identified myself and was abruptly cut off. When I called back I said my name was Grant ... the "Cary" a joke ... and I needed to talk to Mrs. Anderson-Baxter-Edmonds-Landon or Mrs. Landon or whatever name she was using these days. I was asked to call back in twenty minutes. When I did, I was told to call another number and Millie answered on the first ring.

"Cary, what do you want?"

There was no "hello" or "Oh, so nice of you to

call, just icy rhetoric.

"Hey, Mabel slow down, thought I'd drop off your birthday present!"

"Damn it, drop the Mabel! You're not cute! 'Mabel's' not funny! And I don't need a birthday present ... from you!"

"Well, I invested 500 bucks in this bottle of wine I'm holding. It's one of your favorites. What do you want me to do with it?"

"Drink it. Pour it down a sewer. I don't care. Good-bye, Cary!"

"Wait a minute!"

Her sigh was followed by, "What is it with you. You know I don't like you and you insist on calling. Give me a break, get lost!"

"Millie, I'm sorry. Are you still mad that I didn't make any of the funerals? I wasn't in the vicinity when you lost Baxter, Edmonds and Landon. I sent sympathy cards. Hallmark. So you know I care...."

"Cary, you don't care about anything. Good-bye."

I sat there looking at the phone, for a minute or so. It isn't true: I do care about things. Then I walked to the Buena Vista Cafe at Hyde and Beach, and had an Irish coffee. Next, I boarded a Hyde cable car for a ride to Nob Hill. I knew where Millie's condo was located, talked to the door man, and he said Mrs. Landon wasn't in town and had no idea where she was.

I then walked down to Market Street hopped a streetcar and went home. I have an apartment on West Portal. Nothing fancy, but it's all I need to be comfortable. Bed, closet, bathroom, small kitchen ... refrigerator ... a stove and oven I've never used ... microwave, and a huge HD TV unit. I put the wine in the wine rack, and even though it was only 8:00 PM, I showered and went to bed.

Two months later

I was in Sofia, Bulgaria ... in preliminary talks with a small research firm that had, in my estimation, great potential. I'd just finished a two hour presentation on our latest semiconductor do-hickey. A design, I was convinced, held the key to the size, speed, and reliability needed in the project they had outlined weeks before over the internet. As I was leaving their meager facility ... meager compared to most of the facilities that use our products ... my I-Phone rang. It was my ex-wife. Her mother had passed away. The wake was three days away, the funeral, four.

I had no choice. Had to fly back to Minnesota. Margaret Anderson was a good woman. She liked me even though my marriage to her youngest daughter didn't pan out the way everyone had hoped.

I made it to the wake in the evening of my return, when the parlor was crowded with people of every shape, form, color and attire. My ex-father-in-law was standing next to the closed casket, with friends and relatives waiting to console. My ex-wife and her husband were in a small group to one side and Millie was on the other. She had stationed herself in a way to hold back the stream of bodies from overwhelming her father. She was smiling, watching, monitoring progress of the well wishers at the bier.

Our eyes met, less than momentarily, because Millie obviously didn't want to acknowledge my existence. She just kept nodding her head, smiling, saying, "really ... honestly ... no," when the subject changed from what had happened to her mother.

I hung back. Signed the guest book. Put a check in an envelope, and tried to find someone I might know in the crowd. It didn't happen. I knew four people in the room. One was in the casket.

Then, as I stood beside the guest book lectern, my ex saw me and disengaged herself from those around her and came over to greet me.

She smiled the words "Hi Cary," at me.

I gave her a warm hug and said, "I'm so sorry Marjorie. She was a great lady and I loved her ... and I know she loved me, too."

"You're right about that, Cary. You're looking good. Are you okay?"

"Yeah, I'm good. How's the baby? Kids, I mean?"

Marjorie filled me in and it took more than five minutes. Betty is three and a half, Ben going on two. I didn't realize how involved the care and nurturing of two little ones could be, but I soon found out. Then I found out about how her broker husband was doing, and how she was doing and her Dad was doing. I was happy that they were all doing pretty good, up until this point.

"Cary, are you dating anyone?"

"No. No, no ... you know where the job takes me and I'm not around anyone long enough to have any kind of relationship. When you said, 'Good-bye,' that killed the social aspects of my life."

Marjorie took a step back at that and said, "No you don't. I'm not taking a guilt trip for our break up."

"Hey, relax ... it was me, not your fault. I knew, know it was my doing."

It was my doing and it was too late to do anything about it, when she pulled the plug. She had met Mel White at one of Millie's parties. In the course of conversation Mel gave Marjorie a few financial tips. Then kept calling with financial tips and started meeting her with financial tips. The warmth of the meetings and financial tips were the tip of the iceberg in my life. Don't really know if sex was the final argument that brought me the divorce papers and I don't want to know.

Marjorie then smiled and said, "Come along

and talk to Millie and Dad."

Millie said, "Hi," turned and kept the conversation going with the couple of couples she had been talking to. I had been talking to Mr. Anderson for sometime when Millie asked me to move on. Not in those words, but I got the message. I was holding up the receiving line.

I stayed for a few more minutes, and then left.

The next day there was a lunch, held at a nice restaurant, after the memorial service, and a trip to the cemetery. After lunch, I said goodbye and drove the rental car to the Minneapolis-Saint Paul International Airport.

I was getting comfortable and buckling up when Millie came aboard. We were the only two flying first class back to Oakland. I rarely fly into San Francisco. Oakland is easier, although the airport is getting tougher to move around in day by day.

"If I had known you were on this flight, I'd have booked to San Francisco." These were the first words out of Millie's mouth.

"Someday I hope you'll tell me why you hate me so much."

She raised an eyebrow, and said, "Sure. Someday. Nice talking to you." She then curled up in her seat across the aisle and went to sleep.

I read for most of the trip. Millie woke up about an hour away of our destination, went to the john, and then read the in-flight magazine for the rest of the flight.

After leaving the plane, we met again at the luggage carousel. Even though she didn't ask, I watched for her luggage and took it off the merry-go-round. Then I offered to take her home, had a rental reserved. She said no thanks, she would take a cab.

"Look Millie, I'll be happy to take you home. Won't talk. It's on my way. I'll get you right to the door and I'm happy to do it."

"Why?"

"Why not?"

"You know I think less of you than spit."

"Well, no I didn't know that, but the offer stands. I'll get you where you're going and won't say a word."

She had a lot of luggage, and my offer was finally accepted.

I only had a small suitcase and a carryon.

So, I struggled with her three bags and mine. She struggled with her carryon.

****

It was unbelievable ... unbelievable to get a parking spot anywhere near Millie's condo on Nob Hill, but there was one waiting for me, just a car length away from her condo entry.   I don't understand why, but there wasn't a doorman visible, to take Millie's baggage. I'd never been inside her condo. I knew where she lived, but I'd never been invited. Her bags were heavy and not easy to lug to the elevator. Took me two trips.

Once the huffing and puffing subsided, after getting the big, leather baggage inside the living quarters, I was somewhat taken aback by the wall-to-wall magnificence of what Millie had put together here. The entry opened into a hall with the kitchen and a bathroom to the left. A guest bedroom entry was straight ahead. At the other end of the hall was a great room where there was a small dining area and living room. The master bedroom was off the dining area and where Millie wanted her bags put down.

There was lush carpeting, walls painted with swirls and curves of rainbow colors that were remarkably warm and inviting to the eyes. Colorful modern oil paintings and dramatic black and white photography graced the walls. In the living room area, a huge picture window looked out toward San Francisco Bay. All the furniture was expensive, beautiful and the entire condo looked as if no one had ever used it. It looked like the model of a real estate offering, on the first day of showing.

"Wow, your condo is really ... dramatic, beautiful," I said with my head swiveling ... taking it all in.

"Thanks for the ride Cary, and now if you don't

mind, I need some private time."

When she said it, she looked like she was thinking, *"Don't let the door hit you in the ass on your way out!"* So I said so-long, made my exit, and twenty-five minutes later I was in my own pad up on West Portal.

****

I don't why Millie dislikes me so much ... don't have a clue! I do like her, more than she knows. She's a warm, wonderful human being that cares about her family and friends and will go out of her way to help anyone in need ... no matter what the need. I started getting the cold shoulder from her before Marjorie sent me packing. Marjorie, her Dad, and I are friends, but as she said, she thinks less of me than spit.

The first time I saw Millie, when Marjorie brought me home to meet her family, I was pleasantly surprised. Both sisters were beautiful, loved each other, had interesting personalities that complimented one another. I thought if a guy was a Mormon he'd camp out on their doorstep until both women promised to be faithful and loving wives.

Millie was engaged at the time, but she gave the guy walking papers a month before they were to say, "I do." The family was relieved, because the guy had a few quirks that surfaced that eventually would hurt family ties. Family was an important ingredient in the Anderson persona.

My marriage got off to a wonderful start. We got engaged in my senior year at Stanford and were married soon after I started working for HSI. For two years we had fun, enjoyed each other, went everywhere together, when I wasn't working. As I became more successful, the less time I had for Marjorie. Then one day she said we had to talk.

She talked.

I listened.

I packed.

She got what she asked for.

I didn't like it, but I understood.

I was no longer the guy she had married.

I was no longer important in her life.

There was someone else in the picture, too.

•••••••••

Six weeks after the funeral, I flew to London on business. The business only took an hour and half. I found out that my potential customer had already made a commitment to purchase from an arch competitor and I was out in the cold.   And it was cold. The kind of wet and cold December day in London that isn't nice. The cold penetrates to your bones and leaves you with a dismal disposition. I had a warm London hotel room, but not a place where you would want to spend a lot of time. I was booked to stay here for four days.   There were a couple of potential buyers in Europe that I had made arrangements to see, but my appointments were a week away. So, I did some tourist things.

I went to the National Gallery in Trafalgar Square. You could spend a week here, I walked around until closing at 6:00 P.M. Then I went up the street to the Royal George Bar for a drink and something to eat. From there I took a cab to the West End and bought a ticket for the stage version of "Dirty Dancing." I'd seen the movie, thought it might be fun to see what the live musical would be like. As I left my seat during intermission, I got quite a surprise. Marjorie's husband, Mel White was coming out of the men's room, as I was about to enter.

"Mel ... hey ... what are you doing here?"

At first he didn't recognize me, then said, "Cary Grant?"

Now heads were turning, as I said, "Yeah." Then the heads turned again, because obviously things weren't what they had expected, even though the other guy has been dead since 1986.

As we shook hands, Mel said, "Millie gave us, and Dad, a free holiday ride to London. We've been here a week. We're going to Scotland tomorrow. Millie wanted to help Marjorie and Dad get over losing Mom. I believe that Millie is having a tough time, too. It's been really hard on Dad, being alone in Rochester, even though he's always busy at the book store."

I had never called Anders Anderson anything but "Andy." He wasn't my dad and never thought that Andy minded my being informal, but he probably didn't mind Mel calling him Dad either.

"Where are you staying, Mel?"

"We're at a small hotel near Hyde Park, The Gore. It's the place Millie stayed during her first trip to London. Dad is staying with Millie, at her apartment in Mayfair."

"Are they with you now?"

"Marjorie is with me, Millie and Dad didn't want to see this. It's good, don't you think?"

"Yes, I like it. I think the dancing is more interesting than the movie and the movie was great. Mel, do you think we could have coffee or drinks after the show?"

"It's okay with me, Cary. After she gets over the shock of you being here, I'm sure Marjorie would like that, too."

"Swell, I'll meet you in the lobby."

After the "small world" small talk at the theatre was over, we went to the Dog and Duck Pub. It was crowded, but the upstairs room, gave us some elbow room and less noise to contend with.

"So you are going to Scotland tomorrow?" I said, looking at Marjorie over a bitter tasting pint of ale.

"Yes, Millie thought it would be fun. We're

booked on a fast train, traveling first-class and we'll be in Edinburgh two days. We're staying at the Balmoral Hotel. It's close to the train station and said to be quite nice."

"Did you know Millie and I flew home together from Rochester?"

"No ... she never told me."

"We were on the same flight into Oakland. She slept all the way there. Then I gave her a lift home."

"Did you see her condo?"

"Yeah, it's beautiful!"

"I'm surprised she let you inside the door."

"Why is that, Marjorie?"

"I think you know why ... I don't know what you did, but she doesn't like you ... doesn't want to talk about you. For years I've tried to find out what you did or didn't do to cause a problem, but she won't discuss it."

"I've tried to find out, too and she won't give me a clue. I never made any of her husband's funerals, but I think it goes back further than that. Maybe it's my aftershave. Or my politics. I do brush my teeth regularly, shower and shave every day, use deodorant. I "ain't" gonna worry about it."

I told Marjorie and Mel to have a great time in Scotland and that I was heading for Frankfort and Sofia.

"Don't you get tired of traveling?" Marjorie

wanted to know.

"No. The flying is boring, but I enjoy seeing the country side in all the countries I've been blessed to see. I'm taking extra days now in the places I've got customers or potential customers. Time to enjoy the sightseeing."

We broke up after an hour-and-a-half of chitchat.

I spent the next two days going into the nooks and crannies of London; Windsor, Berkshire; Maidenhead, and Slough. So much to see. I'll have to come back another day. I would like to visit Horfield, Bristol sometime, where my namesake was born and raised.

... on a train to Edinburgh ...

Mr. Anderson and Mel are sitting together. A few seats away, Marjorie and Millie are side by side.

"Millie, why don't you like Cary?"

"You don't want to know, Marjorie!"

"Yes, I do. I still have some affection for him, he's a good guy, not one I want to spend my life with, but basically a good guy.   If he had had more interest in our relationship and had wanted kids, I probably never would have left him."

"He's not as good as you think, Marjorie."

"What do you mean by that?"

"Let's not talk about it, you'll just be upset."

"I'm upset now. What do you mean?"

"Cary Grant is a philanderer. He probably has women everywhere he stops on the selling trail."

"I don't believe what I'm hearing. How can you say that? Do you mean he was hitting on you when I was married to him?"

"I knew I shouldn't get into this conversation. No, he never hit on me. I did see him hitting on someone at the Oakland airport ... a year before you left him. He had his arms around a nice looking woman and kissed her ... well, it wasn't a brotherly buss. It was one of the red, hot kisses you used to talk about when you first started dating him. I almost went over and hit him in the head with the umbrella I was carrying. Then I thought you'd defend the SOB, and never talk to me again."

"I don't believe it. He was never that way. I'd have known!"

"Why did he leave you go so easily, when you told him you were through with him?"

Marjorie was looking out of the train window now, lost in thought. Finally she said, "It wasn't easy for him. He couldn't believe that I was leaving him. Couldn't believe I was seeing Mel. Couldn't believe he was that bad a husband. He told me he wouldn't make waves.   He packed up and left. Gave me the rights to the house and everything in it. Gave me the car, the savings account, the stock portfolio. He kept what was in the checking account, but that was it. The lawyer that Mel had set me up with couldn't believe Cary. He signed away everything. Didn't read he papers. Didn't tell me where he could be reached. I called his office to thank him, but he wouldn't take the call. He finally called after I married Mel and wished me well. I asked if we could still be friends and he said yes. But as you know, he doesn't keep in touch. I don't doubt what you saw, Millie, but there has to be some explanation. He didn't, wouldn't do anything to hurt me, I'm sure of it."

"Well, believe what you will, I think he's bad news!"

The two said nothing more for the rest of the train ride.

****

After spending a couple of days in Frankfurt and Sophia, I headed for home. The trips had been time well spent. I learned that the products I had left with the Sophia organization were working out well. I was told that some modifications were necessary, but I knew these were of a type that wouldn't take long to produce. After checking with headquarters, I learned that the modified product could be scheduled for production in four to five weeks and the cost would be slightly less than our original quotation. Things were looking up.

I had been back in San Francisco two weeks when Marjorie called me at work and asked if I would be available for lunch. She was doing some shopping in town and would like to have some company. I did have luncheon plans, but the kind that could easily be rescheduled, so I said sure. We met at a nice, quiet place on Van Ness at noon. Have to admit I was curious. This was a first. After our divorce, I'd never been alone with Marjorie anywhere. She was already seated when I arrived.

"Hi," I said as I slid into the booth across from her.

"Hello, Cary. Thanks for coming."

"What's this all about? Where are your kids?"

"My mother-in-law has them." Then we talked for a while about what happened in London, Scotland and Ireland while across the water with her Dad and Millie. A good time was had by all. She asked about my days on the sales trail.

Then...

"I found out why Millie doesn't like you much."

"Oh, why is that? Happy the mystery is over and what do I have to do to get back in her good graces."

"She thinks you were two-timing me, when we were married."

"What ... what makes her think that? Never did

but I am curious about where she got that idea."

"She said she saw you kissing a woman at the Oakland airport when we were married. Said it was one of your red hot kisses."

I sat there, momentarily stunned. Drawing a complete blank about giving a *red, hot kiss* to anyone except Marjorie while I was married.

"I never gave Millie a red, hot kiss so I don't know how she could be a judge, and who was it I was supposed to be kissing?"

"I told her I didn't believe it. She said it was a year before our divorce. The woman left your arms and boarded a plane and then you left. Millie was on the other side of the waiting area. She was flying to Rochester that day."

"I can't imagine ... wait a minute. Do you remember the time I had lunch with Terri, the girl I went steady with in high-school. She was visiting friends in Walnut Creek. Called me before going home to Waverly. Asked if we could have lunch? Do you remember me telling you about that? Probably not, it was years ago."

"Oh, yes. I do recall that. I was more than a bit jealous. Thought you could have called and asked me to join you. I do remember that."

"Terri and I were very close. When she left that day, she did give me a kiss ... and it was one of *her* red, hot kisses. The kind she used to give me with her arms wrapped around my neck and legs off the ground, locked behind my back. No legs were locked at the airport, but the kiss was every bit one to remember. I didn't tell you about that ... knew you wouldn't appreciate my enjoyment. It was one of those memories you savor. When school ended, she went to Iowa State, not far from Waverly, I went to Stanford, where I met you and thought I'd live happily ever after. She married, and as far as I know, she is living happily ever after."

"You bum!"

"Me?"

"You don't have to enjoy telling me that so much!"

"Hey, lady ... I've never asked how you became so enamored with Mel before we split. And no, I don't want to know. That was your doing, not mine and I'm sure there must have been a few 'red hot kisses' mixed in with who knows ... well, only you and Mel know ...and lets keep it that way, okay."

"Cary, I'm still amazed at how you just got up and left when I told you we were through. You have a temper. I thought you would break windows, yell and scream, hit me or burn the house down. But, you calmly packed up and left."

"Well, I thought about doing those things. Then ... you were sitting there with tears in your eyes, lower lip quivering ... I thought about my contribution to the situation. I was gone a lot. Many times I was thinking

about my next sales call, when I should have been concentrating on what you were saying. I went out with
the guys a lot when I should have been taking you
places. You didn't complain until the day you said, 'so
long' and then it was too late. Do you know what I did
after leaving the house that day?"

"What?"

"I drove to Sausalito. Walked back to the
Golden Gate. Walked to the middle of the bridge and
tossed my wedding ring over the side. Then I heaved
the watch you gave me as an anniversary present over
the side, after which I stuffed the contents of the bill-
fold you gave me in my pockets and tossed it in the
drink. When the final paper work was done, I got rid of
everything you ever gave me and tried my damnedest
to forget about you.   That didn't work, but at least I
had no reminders left to deal with."

"Oh, Cary, I'm so sorry."

"No, you aren't. You have a caring husband and
two wonderful kids. That's a hell of a lot more than I
came away with."

There were a few more minutes of small talk
and then we went our separate ways. Again.

****

A week after having lunch with Marjorie, I found out that HSI had been sold to XXO Corp., a huge conglomerate. HSI was to be absorbed into their SemiXX Division. It turned out that the HSI commission system didn't agree with the way things were done at SemiXX. I was making more money than their VP of sales and VP of marketing combined. So, I was out of a job.

I came away with my 401K intact, my last commission check, but not a fond farewell. It didn't matter. I incorporated under the name CG Enterprises, Ltd. Then I networked myself into being a rep for a small but innovative developer of microprocessors and GPUs, and signed up to rep a few microelectronic equipment manufacturers. Then I had a Home Page developed complete with short videos of the products and equipment in my new bag of tricks. The videos gleaned from parts and pieces of videos used by companies I represent.

Next I contacted Dun & Bradstreet. They offer ways to identify key executives in the markets I'm interested in. I wanted to make my presence felt and needed some help in developing sales leads. I know many of my prospects, but there are a vast number out there that I have never called on. I have no overhead, no one to answer to, and my passport has plenty of room for going anywhere I choose. I get paid on delivery and I'm not about to starve. My connections are excellent, my networking is in place and this Cary Grant's star quality is pretty good, if I do say so myself.

Another bright spot in my new situation, spring is in the air. Trees are budding, flowers are pushing skyward, and people are becoming friendly again along West Portal and in San Francisco, in general. For some unknown reason, I wanted to talk to Millie. Tell her how wrong she had been about me, that I didn't deserve her wrath and should be regarded quite a bit above the value of spit. I called her cell and was told that the number was no longer in service. I thought about calling her answering service, but didn't and I don't know why. Instead, I called a couple of buddies and we went to a bar on Broadway for a couple of drinks, sight seeing, and wound up at the Buena Vista near the Wharf. Their Irish Coffee is the best anywhere. Don't know how they keep on delivering the same consistency night after night, day after day, but I really don't care. I had two, as we talked, then I caught a cable car for Market Street and a streetcar home. Once there, I did call Millie's answering service. They told me she was no longer a customer.

****

I had started making calls to my long list of HSI customers to inform them that I no longer represented the company. When I joined HSI, I was forced to sign a non-compete agreement. Now that HSI no longer existed, as it was, I had no compunction about living up to the 'non-compete.' I had developed some strong business relationships and friends along the way and they welcomed my calls. I found out that doing business with SemiXX wasn't as rewarding as it had been with HSI, when I had been there. This gave me the incentive to get back on the travel trail. Showing up at the door steps of past customers made good business sense, and provided the opportunity to show all the "new stuff" in my bag of tricks.

I decided to make London my first stop and knew it would be a good place to set up my European appointments. Since Mel and Marjorie seemed to think that the Gore Hotel was nice, I made reservations there. I arrived after 5:00 PM, and found the accommodations comfortable. When I signed the register, the wise guy at the desk wanted to know if they could use my name in advertising. You know, Cary Grant is staying at the Gore, that type of thing. I declined the opportunity.

When my bags were unpacked, I plopped down on the bed, and grabbed the telephone book. I started looking for the home phone of Tyler Andre, a good friend and buyer that I have known for more than a few years. I wanted company for dinner, I knew his business number, but not his home phone. Tyler is a bachelor and enjoys Scotch, good food and conversation. As my finger skipped down the page, it abruptly stopped at a very familiar name: Millicent Anderson in Mayfair. If she hadn't been using her maiden name in the directory, I wouldn't have thought about calling. But I did call, thinking wouldn't it be nice if Millie were in London and hadn't eaten as yet. After three rings, she answered.

"Hello."

"Hi, Millie. How are you?"

"Who is this ... Cary? Cary Grant?"

"Yes, it's me."

"What are you doing here? Are you in London? Here?"

"Yes, I'm making sales calls in Europe. Just got in."

"I don't need anything, Cary."

"Nice comeback. Quick. I was just wondering if you would have dinner with me."

"How did you know I was here?"

"I was looking for a friend of mine in the phone book. Tyler Andre. Saw your name and forgot about calling Tyler."

"Well, why don't you call your friend now. I'm sure he would enjoy your company."

"For Pete's sake, Millie, haven't you talked to Marjorie. What you saw ..."

"Sounded like a fairy tale to me, Cary, one of your adept sales pitches. You aren't married anymore, why didn't you just fess up and be done with it?"

"I did 'fess up.' What I told Marjorie is exactly what happened," and there was more than a trace of irritation in my words.

Millie came back with, "Cary call your friend Tyler. I'm sorry, I can't have dinner with you, I'm busy."

"That's a brush off, Millie. Why?"

"You're right, though I really am busy. Where are you staying? If you're still in London on Thursday, I'll have dinner with you. I'll have to break another date, so give me your number."

"I'm at the Gore. You have the number. I'll be here Thursday."

"Okay, bye for now." She hung up before I could say anything.

I did reach Tyler and we made a night of it. Ate at a good, quiet, restaurant, then went to a popular multi-room night spot in Greenwich that played loud music until our ears were sated, eyes filled, and heads groggy. It was a good night. When we left, rain was falling and the streets of London reflected neon patterns that looked like a museum filled with the kind of kinetic sculpture that makes your head swim.

****

On Thursday morning, Millie called. She said

she couldn't talk long, but she had picked a spot for dinner. She picked a Turkish restaurant in London's West End. Set the time for 8:00 PM. Didn't give me any details, other than the time and place. When I arrived at the restaurant at 7:55 PM, Millie was already seated ... along with six other women. They were all pretty, and charming ... well, they were very decorative to say the least. I was introduced, and everyone enjoyed cocktails, and appetizers, with small talk. The "getting to know you" kind of small talk. No one believed my name was Cary Grant when introduced, but Millie did confirm it. Before, the main entree was served I realized that these fine ladies were not Millie's friends, they were "hired escorts." They were all smiling, and acted as if they were looking forward to what was to come. As the servers were carefully presenting the main course for our enjoyment, I excused myself, saying I had to make a trip to the men's room. Instead, I went to the bar area, found our waiter, wrote a brief note, saying, *Millie, thanks for the 'whore d'oeuvres.'* Then I asked for the check, told the waiter to add in dessert for everyone, paid the bill and left.

But the night wasn't over.

As I walked out of the door of the restaurant, it was pouring, and I saw a cab parked on the opposite side of the street. So I lunged off the curb, started running, and ran right into the oncoming path of one of those beautiful double-decker London buses. The driver did what was expected, stomped on his brakes, but the bus refused to stop as quickly as necessary, and I wound up face down on the street with a broken arm, concussion and facial damage ... I left about a pound of flesh off the good side of my face on a rain soaked London thoroughfare.

A hospital lorry was dispatched and I woke up in the emergency room of St. Luke's Hospital for the Clergy. I wasn't wearing my ecclesiastic collar so I have no idea why I was where I was. When I asked, it seems there had been a number of accidents at the appointed hour of my arrival and the ambulance had been directed here. My head hurt, my arm hurt, my face hurt, and they graciously put me under while they attended to my broken arm, cuts and bruises.

When I awoke, I actually felt better than when they put me to sleep. My head had a dull pain, but I've had a number of hangovers that were far worse. I was no longer the handsome guy I was yesterday. My arm throbbed a bit. It was in a cast, and I wasn't thrilled about it. My right arm is an asset that you don't want to part with ... responsible for so many things we take for granted, that I started to hyperventilate, thinking about what I wouldn't be able to do for a while.

The good doctors kept me another day, wanted to make sure the concussion didn't keep my head swimming. They told me that my arm should take about three to four weeks to heal. After leaving the clergy behind, I took a cab back to the Gore. When I arrived, the man at the desk told me that two lovely women had come to the hotel two nights before, looking for me. When I didn't return by 2:00 A.M., they left a note and went on their way.

The note said, *Mr. Grant: We owe you one. Please call. Ask for Gloria or Cassandra.* A card for an escort service was attached to the note.

I didn't call.

****

The next morning I left for Sofia, Bulgaria and called on six prospects there. After that I spent close to a month knocking on doors in Germany, Denmark and Sweden. I didn't sell much, but did find some opportunities that I felt would pay off down the road. Looking like I'd been run over by a bus made it easy to start most conversations, and the products I offered looked interesting to most of the men and women I had meetings with. When I returned to London, I went back to the hospital and had the cast removed. I felt like celebrating. Had two hands back that made zipping zippers and buttoning buttons easy once again.

****

Have you ever watched the movie, *'An Affair to Remember'*? I'll bet you have seen it a number of times. I didn't book a reservation on the Queen Mary 2 because my name is Cary Grant and wanted to see if Deborah Kerr was on board. The ship was in the harbor, set to leave, had a room available in steerage, and I was not in a hurry to get anywhere. So I thought, 'what the hell,'and sailed.

If you believe that *Fate is a Hunter,* like the novel by Ernest Gann, it won't surprise you that Millie was on board, too. With the ship's capacity for handling 2,600 passengers, I didn't find her on the cruise. I found her by accident, as we disembarked. She had been staying in a top deck suite for the very rich. I had been comfortable, but not nearly as comfortable as Millie.

I was about ten steps behind her as we got off the boat, moving toward the baggage area. She is very easy to recognize from the front, side or rear ... and as I was watching her rear end moving movements, I knew it was Millie. No one walks like Millie in high heels. When I managed to get right behind her, I said, "That was a dirty trick, Millie."

She didn't faint hearing my voice, but turned abruptly and said, "No! Cary, what are you doing here?" The look on her face was bewildered to say the least.

"I could ask you the same question, but know

you weren't following me. How are your friends?"

"What friends?"

"Your girl friends. The only two I remember are Cassandra and Gloria."

"I'll bet!"

"They left a note, when I didn't get back to the hotel. Said to call, but I declined. How much did that hoax cost?"

"Didn't get back to the hotel? What are you talking about?"

"I went right from the restaurant to St. Luke's Hospital for the Clergy. There were no last-rites, but I did stay a few days. How much did you pay those hookers?"

"Were you sick? Is that why you left? How much do I owe you for dinner?"

"You don't owe me a thing."

"Why the hospital? You're kidding right?"

"No, I got hit by a bus."

"No!"

"Yep. Right outside the restaurant. About the time you were taking the first bite of food. Was the food good?"

"What happened?"

"I didn't want to eat with your friends. Paid the bill. Left. It was raining, pouring actually. Saw a cab, didn't see the bus. Wound up with a broken arm, concussion, cuts and bruises. I'm happy my face and arm have healed nicely."

"Really, you're not kidding. You got hit by a bus?"

"Oh yes. If you look close, I still have blotches where my face played slip and slide with the pavement. You know, that dinner thing was a dirty trick!"

"Yes, I do know. I thought you'd call and give me hell. Was surprised you didn't."

We were now in the baggage area. "What are you doing after going through Customs," I asked.

"I'm going to my Condo. I'm meeting a real estate woman there. I'm going to sell it."

"Where is it located?"

"It's on the upper east side on Park Avenue, a 2-bedroom apartment. Would you like to see it?"

I'll admit it. I've been trying to get close to Millie since Marjorie gave me the heave ho ... trying to find out why she doesn't like me, so I could repair the damage, and now I know. I didn't want to tear up my plane ticket to Oakland in front of her, but there was no way I was about to pass up her invitation. As nonchalantly as I could, I said, "Sure." I hoped my tongue wasn't hanging out or that she could tell I was breathing hard and my hands were sweating.

Millie said, "Fine, Wait when you get through Customs."

We didn't say much in the taxi on the way to the condo. I was enjoying the view. Millie is beautiful!

After getting past the doorman, we rode the elevator up, up, and away to reach our destination. The entry door opened on a luxurious setting. The condo had three exposures ... north, south and east ... a high ceiling, a decorative fireplace, and parquet wood floors. The small windowed kitchen had a number of nice feminine touches. I thought it was a warm, comfortable place for anyone who liked New York City living. Millie was a bit uncomfortable. She had lived here for two years with her last husband. Now, she was about to purge it from her memory and I think it was the reason she asked me along. She didn't want to be alone here.

"Cary, the real estate woman should be here in about an hour. Then I have someone from an auction house coming tomorrow, and I've asked the Salvation Army to send someone over tomorrow afternoon. Would you mind staying here with me until tomorrow?"

"No, I can do that." I didn't say I'd love to. If she had looked at me closely, that would have been apparent.

The real estate woman spent about twenty minutes looking at all the rooms, nooks and crannies and told Millie that she would recommend setting a price of one million-nine for the condo. She explained that prospects would counter with a price of somewhere between one million two or three. That would make a compromise of one million five acceptable. She said that one million five was what she felt the property was worth. Millie liked the woman, signed the sales agreement and we all went to lunch. The woman took us to the Russian Tea Room, and recommended the caviar omelette and that is what we ordered. The women had a glass of white wine and I had a beer.

After lunch Millie and I went to the Ground Zero Museum, then the Metropolitan Museum of Art. We took our time, talked as we walked, and I felt that Millie was warming up to having me around.

When Marjorie and I first married, the three of us had many great times together. Fun times. Enjoyed being together. When Millie married we didn't get together as often and then ... all of a sudden ... she began distancing herself from us. Now, knowing that she felt I was cheating on her sister, everything was understandable.

We tarried long enough in the museums that it was time for dinner when we walked out of the Metropolitan Museum of Art. So, we hailed a cab and went to Rock Center Cafe. It's on the North side of the skating rink in Rockefeller Center. Millie said it had been a favorite of her husband. During dinner, since I didn't know much of anything about the men she had married, I asked her about them. She reminisced a bit and said all three were very loving spouses, all different, enjoyed different things.

Then she asked me about Terri. I think she was

still in a disbelieving mode about how faithful I had been. I explained Terri was a cute cheerleader in high school when I had played football. We started dating when we were seniors. Her dad was the football coach. Even though we were a steady twosome, we both knew that when school ended, our relationship would end. She went to Iowa State, I went to Stanford. Other than in the airport, I hadn't seen her since my Mom and Dad were killed in an auto accident coming home from Waterloo. I was in my sophomore year at Stanford when it had happened.

After dinner we went back to the condo. Talked some more over a glass of French Chardonnay before retiring. I woke at 7:00 A.M. as usual, had a warm shower, shaved and dressed. When I entered the kitchen, Millie was not only dressed but had eggs on the stove, bacon frying, plates and silverware on the table with a copy of the Wall Street Journal nestled against a toaster there.

"Holy smoke, where did you get the eggs and bacon?"

"I went to the store. I lived here for two years you know. Made breakfast most mornings. How do you like your eggs? Talk fast, they're almost done."

"I like 'em runny, bacon crisp, coffee black, thank you."

"Well sit down, we're ready to eat then."

"How did you know I'd be here when every

thing was ready?"

"Heard the shower quit. Knew it wouldn't take very long for you to shave and dress. Good guess, right?"

"Perfect!"

"Cary, I have a man from the Sotheby Auction House coming at nine, after that someone from the Salvation Army will be here. I plan to fly to Green Bay this afternoon."

"Green Bay?"

"Yes, I have a home ... a condo ... in Door County, near Green Bay, that I want to sell. I've never seen it. It belonged to Lee. I'd like to ask for another favor, but I don't want to interfere with your business. If you can't do it, I'll understand."

"Can't do what Millie? What are you asking?"

"If you can afford the time, I'd like you to come with me to Door County. I'm a little apprehensive. When Lee died, I didn't want to go there. It's been shut for over three years. I pay the taxes, the charges for services, but I don't know what shape it's in and I'd like someone with me when I find out. I was going to ask Marjorie, until you happened along. If you can't or don't want to do it, I'll understand."

The phone rang at that moment. It was the doorman announcing that a man named Markey, from Sotheby was asking for her.

"Please send him on, Jim. Thank you," Then

she put down the phone and went to the entry to let the man in. She explained to Mr. Markey that she was selling the condo and there were a number of paintings and artifacts that she wanted sold. She gave him a tour, pointing out what she thought might be of interest to Sotheby, and Markey made notes. A few things were not of interest, mostly furniture type items, but he said he would definitely get back to her.

She told the man that she wanted the things removed from the premises after the sale of the property. That she would be in San Francisco in a week, and she gave him her cell number. As Markey was going out the door, the phone rang again and the Salvation Army had arrived. The reason Millie called, she told the new arrival, some items would be available when the condo was sold. If the Army wasn't interested in them they would be have to be junked. She had a list, with the Sotheby items crossed off, and asked if the Salvation Army would be interested in a donation of this type. The answer was affirmative. She said someone would call when the things could be picked up, but she didn't know when that would be. The Salvation Army man assured her this was no problem.

When the door closed on the last visitor, I looked at Millie and told her I would be happy to travel with her to Door County. She was visibly delighted, smiling, and said, "Oh Cary, thank you so much. I really, really appreciate it!"

I was hoping she would throw her arms around me, kiss me and stay puckered long enough for me to kiss her back. It didn't happen, but I was making progress. I got a *'thank you so much, I really, really appreciate it!'* And I was invited to travel with her, and I didn't think she would be sleeping all the way to Green Bay.

****

We managed to get two first class seats on a Northwest flight. Just managed to make the flight and landed in Green Bay at 5:00 PM. The car rental took about ten minutes, and an hour-and-a-half later we were in Sister Bay ... and Millie's Condo. The place had a wonderful view of the bay, two bedrooms, great room, dining area, small kitchen, two baths, and a boat slip about thirty yards from the back door. The place was musty from standing idle for such a long time, and Millie didn't want to stay, but we did look around and there were some personal things of Lee in evidence, that Millie found difficult to see.

"I'll have to come back tomorrow and clean out Lee's personal stuff, air the place out and find a real estate agent," Millie said. She wasn't talking to me, but I understood what was going through her mind.

"Let's get out of here and find a motel," I said, as I headed for the door. Millie picked up the Condo's phone book as we made our exit, and even though it wasn't the height of the tourist season, it took three calls to find two rooms. The place was in Ephraim, just down the road from Sister Bay. We had passed the motel on the way in. The rooms were nice, not lavish, but nice. They were on the second floor. After freshening up, I checked for places to eat on my I-Phone and came up with The Inn at Kristofer's in Sister Bay. I called and made a reservation for two and was told I'd have a half hour wait after arriving. Didn't matter. The place has floor to ceiling windows, a beautiful view of the bay and while waiting another couple told us the food was fantastic. It turned out that it was.

****

I had some trouble sleeping. Got up at 5:30 and checked my home page on my laptop. Had four orders to process. The process being, I sent the orders to my suppliers and asked them to notify me when the orders were shipped. Two people wanted my presence. One was Motorola in Schaumburg, Illinois. The other a small company in Vancouver, British Columbia. They had left their numbers. After breakfast, Millie and I went back to the condo. While she was busy tossing things in garbage bags, I made my calls and set up appointments.

The real estate woman that Millie contacted had

known Millie's husband Lee. She arrived about five minutes after Millie had put her phone back in her purse. As the two talked, I made reservations to fly to Chicago and Vancouver.

As we drove back to Green Bay, Millie told me that the real estate agent had three prospects for her property, three that really wanted a condo near the water, so selling Lee's place wouldn't take long. Since all the furniture was in good shape, the woman felt the offering should be marketed 'as is,' which would save Millie a lot of trouble. While we drove, Millie made a reservation for San Francisco, through O'Hare which meant we would be flying together once again.

When we landed, Millie had only an hour to kill before her flight back to the coast. Getting to my appointment at Motorola on time meant I had to rent a car and leave O'Hare as quickly as possible. That meant saying so long to Millie at her gate.

"Take care of yourself, Cary."

"You too!"

"Call me when you get back in town."

"You mean that?"

"Yes."

"Oh, I'll call, you can bet on it."

With that, Millie moved in close to me, gave me a quick, friendly, good-bye kiss and said, "You better run."

I wanted more than that peck she delivered, but

I did have to run. As I hurried off, I savored the trace of lip stick on my mouth, the scent of her hair that lingered, the image of her beautiful eyes looking at me at that moment when our lips parted. I imagined that the look said, *"Let's do this again."* You can't trust imagination.

****

The interview at Motorola went well. I didn't make a sale, but knew what I had to offer was in the ball park for one, when they made a final decision. As I left Schaumburg, I had more than enough time to make my flight to Vancouver. I had booked my flight on Alaska Airlines, and made a reservation for a room at the Pan Pacific Hotel. The four and a half hour flight was on time and we landed at 7:30 P.M. My room at the hotel was on the eighteenth floor overlooking mountains, and cruise ships coming and going in the Burrard Inlet. Nice. I unpacked my bag, ordered from room service, ate and went to bed.

The next morning was more than I had bargained for. I met my prospective clients in their offices at 9:30 A.M.   Two young men and I sat around a scarred wooden table, not much bigger than one you might play poker on, in a room about the size of a two car garage. A room cluttered with benches holding electronic monitors and gizmos and a mess of materials, tools, small cabinets, boxes and more clutter. On the table, in front of us, was a shaft about a yard long, the upper part of which was enclosed in a golf grip. The lower portion incorporated a fixture about a foot long and a few inches wide that contained a number of buttons. I judged that my potential customers were about twenty to twenty-five years old and exuberant, to say the least. Jake Harmon, a tall blond with a crew cut and glasses, and Keith Landowski, a somewhat shorter guy, with a week old beard, long blond hair and deep set blue eyes ... were both talking at once, pointing, waving their arms, so I said, "Whoa, gentlemen ... please slow down ... I'm having a hard time following."

"Cary, we're electronic engineering students and Keith here ... Keith had this crazy idea and we're both convinced it will make millions. We need some help, and advice, and a friend recommended we contact you." Jake sputtered as he grabbed the shaft and handed it to me.

"Who's the friend," I wanted to know.

"Mel White, he's one of my Dad's friends. Went to school with him," Jake told me.

"Okay. I know Mel. What is this thing, what does it do?"

"It's a golf swing tutoring device ... game ... practice instrument ... all rolled into one.

"Looks a little clumsy, to me."

"That's why we need you."

"Better explain the whole process, I'm a bit of

a skeptic. I play golf and I don't see why you guys are so excited."

The golf club they envisioned, would enable a golfer to choose a driver, putter, and all the clubs in between with the touch of a button. Then practice his swing using laser and integrated circuit technology. "Swing feel and sound of impact" were a part of the package. The system was interfaced with a DVD that delivered progressive, hole by hole views of a prestigious golf course. They were using Pebble Beach golf course to demonstrate.

Depending on a golfer's swing, a slice, hook, perfect, near-perfect or not so perfect shot would occur. A golf ball image on the screen would travel distances related to the theoretical impact, that was registered electronically as the shaft's laser club face "hit" a stationary teed up ball ... a ball on a mat a few yards away from the television monitor. When finally on the green, you hit the putter button, addressed the ball and then putted. The program kept your score on a projected score card in the corner of the TV monitor. I was fascinated. I'd never played Pebble Beach and it appeared I was about to get my chance.

These guys were looking for help to get more miniaturization and capabilities into the design of "the club" and had specific areas where they needed help. The initial design didn't feel quite right when you made the swing movement. I'm a salesman, not a design engineer, but I do know semi-conductor capabilities and what's available, so I thought I'd lend a hand. I was in Vancouver for more than a week ... talking ... listening ... calling my suppliers ... getting answers ...waiting for answers ... getting more involved than I usually do on customer projects. But how often does a guy get to play Pebble Beach without emptying his wallet?

During the evenings, I explored Vancouver and found that I really like the place. I had rented a Jeep ... a Wrangler ... and bumped over some back-roads, and city streets.   I talked to Millie a number of times when she wasn't busy.   The last time we talked, on the day I was leaving, she said she was in Bend. Bend, Oregon at her home in the Sun River Resort complex.

"How long have you been there?" I asked.

"Just arrived," she told me.

"How long are you staying?

"I'll be here a couple of weeks. How's everything going in Vancouver?"

"I've done all I can do at this point. The guys are going back to the drawing board and have more work to do that I can't help them with. I'm leaving here today."

"Well, have a safe trip home ... have to go, a friend is waiting. I'm playing golf. Not beautiful Pebble Beach, but a nice course, nevertheless."

"Keep your head down."

"So long, Cary," and she was gone.

I felt like calling her back. Thought she probably would have turned her phone off and I'd be wasting my time.

Then I did the most irrational thing I've done in quite a while. I canceled my flight. Returned my rental, took a cab to a Jeep dealer and bought a Wrangler off the floor. It is a bright red, two-door, stick shift, top of the line Wrangler. Newer and more luxurious than the rental I'd been rolling around in.

I don't need a car in San Francisco. I use public transportation, cab it, or rent wheels when needed. So this wasn't a sane exercise. It was an extravagance, and part of a plan that was formulating inside my adventurous head.

****

It doesn't take long to reach the border from Vancouver. I had to wait about five minutes at the I-5, Peace Arch crossing. I'd never driven across Washington, and it is beautiful. Pine trees, greenery, mountains, lakes, beauty is everywhere. I made a detour off I-5 and drove onto Whidbey Island, over the Deception Pass bridge and wound up in Mukilteo where a ferry will take you back to the mainland. Enjoyed the short ferry ride. A short time later I was back on I-5 and battling Seattle traffic. Didn't stop in Seattle, just kept on going south at a snails pace until I passed Tacoma.

Mt. Rainier was visible most of the way, in all its snow capped splendor. It took me about eight hours to reach Portland ... about three hours longer than it should have taken since I had to wait for a ferry, and eat and made a couple of pit stops along the way. I found a motel on the South side of Portland and spent the night. I was up bright and early the next day. Drove to Eugene and turned east for the trip over the mountains toward Bend. It took me two and a half hours to get there.

****

The Sun River Resort Lodge did have a room. Someone had canceled one and it was available for four days. It was busy time in Sun River. I booked all the available days, happy as a lark. Then I poked my I-Phone for restaurant info and it looked like a place called the Pine Tavern would be a good spot to eat. It was only about twenty miles away. So that's where I went for an early lunch. I found the food good, coffee strong, and the atmosphere pleasing.

After paying the check, I walked out the door, and there she was walking toward me. Dressed in a tennis outfit that emphasized all the structural components that made Millie so easy on the eyes. She was talking to a tennis friend as she walked and there were two male counterparts to the foursome just a few steps behind.

As her head turned toward me and recognized who was on the walk in front of her, she shouted my name. "Cary! Cary, you're here! What's going on?" The look on her face was bewildered to say the least, and from the sound of her voice I couldn't tell if she happy to see me, or about to have a stroke.

"Just thought I might take a few days off from the business trail ... thought I might run into a beautiful blonde somewhere on my sojourn south," I answered.

Blushing a bit, she went to great lengths to introduce me to her friends and let them know that I was her sister's ex-husband. It was apparent that her friend Howie wasn't interested in meeting Cary Grant. After a cursory handshake he and his buddy Kevin walked around us and said they would get a table.

"Cary, how long will you be here?"

"Well, I've got a room at the Lodge booked for four days. They're booked up."

With that her friend Cherie excused herself, and went to join the men in the restaurant.

"If I had known, I would have planned this holiday much differently," Millie said.

"How differently?"

"Well, Howie, Kevin, Cherie and I came up here together. We play golf and tennis regularly. The guys are staying at the Lodge, Cherie is staying with me. If I had known what you were planning, I'd have had those three come up next week and we ... you and I ... could have played some golf together."

"How long will they be here?"

"For three more days ... and that's when you leave. Nuts!"

"I don't have any trips planned, my business is in good shape. If I can find a room somewhere, I'll stay longer. And I won't intrude on your friends. "

"You mean it?"

"Yes, I mean it. Are you and Howie an item? He looked like he doesn't want to share, and I can understand why he'd feel that way."

"Cary, stop selling. Howie would like more of a relationship, but there's nothing going on between us. He's just a guy I'm comfortable with ... playing golf and tennis. Oh, we do other things ... once in a while ... usually with Kevin and Cherie. The four of us have known each other for some time."

There was a slight pause at the end of that sentence, and then she said, "Don't look for another place to stay, Cary, you can stay with me. I have two bedrooms. Cherie and I can share one."

"Swell. I won't horn in on your friends. I'll see you Monday."

"I'm looking forward to it." Then, before I could turn away, she moved in and gave me a kiss. Another friendly kiss, but much warmer than a brotherly type of smooch this time. I thought: Wow! ... among other things, and wished Monday was tomorrow. As I drove back to the Sun River Lodge, I sang all the way.

****

The next days were a drag. Not entirely. On Friday I drove down to Crater Lake, about ninety miles south of Sun River. The lake is blue and beautiful. Six miles wide. The result of a volcanic eruption and collapse several thousand years ago. It's one of our oldest National Parks and truly a sight to see. On Saturday, I rented a bike and pedaled all around Sun River.

My expectations of what Monday would bring, ran the gamut of human experience. Up and down, down and up again. I felt like a teenager ... in the mood for love and worried that I would say the wrong things, make the wrong moves, fumble opportunities, wind up on Millie's hate list once again. I tried hard to relax, but I was a basket case. So, after my bike ride and shower, I decided to sit in the Lodge bar, sip a drink and eat whatever the establishment used to keep bar sitters bending their elbows. I'd only taken my first sip when....

Millie tapped me on the shoulder and sat down on the bar stool next to mine.

"Hi," was all she said.

The lump in my throat got in the way of my answer for more than a few seconds. Her hair was pulled back in a ponytail, her face was radiant, she smelled shower fresh with just a hint of a special fragrance and I had to fight hard against my inclination to reach out and grab hold of her.

"Where are your friends?" was the best I could do at a comeback.

"I sent them on their way, said I wasn't feeling well and that they should head back to the city."

"You're sick?"

"No, dummy. I wanted to be with you. After I saw you at the restaurant, I knew you came to Sun River just for me. I kept thinking about that. And you. Thinking about the good times we had when you were married to Marjorie. Up until, you know when.

"I love Marjorie, but in retrospect I think I was jealous of her happiness when she was married to you. Then I hated you because I thought you were cheating on her. Since being around you ... since coming back to the States, I've more than changed my mind. You've never made a move to show me how you feel about me, but I think I know. If I'm wrong, please tell me now, because I want more of you than holding hands. Am I wrong about the way you feel?"

"I only have one question."

"What's that?"

"Where do you want to go on our honeymoon?"

For a second she was startled ...and then she

smiled, grinned, giggled, and broke into laughter. Laughed and laughed some more. When she recovered she answered, "We're not going skiing, or on a bike ride in Hawaii, and you are going to take a complete physical before I say I do."

"How about a cruise to London?"

"Only if you promise we won't go out on deck."

And that my friends is the story of how I got Millie for a wife, retired early, and have no doubt that I'll live happily ever after. As my Hollywood name-sake, Cary Grant once said, "I'm Mr. Lucky!"

****

.

...

About the author

Dan Glaubke was born and raised in Chicago on the northwest side. He joined the U.S. Army during the Korean War, graduated from U.S. Army Intelligence School, Ft. Riley, Kansas, and was stationed in Germany for most of his enlistment. His professional life includes being an advertising copywriter for The Buchen Company and Fensholt Incorporated, both business-to-business advertising agencies. He served as Creative Director, President and CEO of Fensholt from 1974 to 1995. He's been happily married for 58 years, has three married children and six grandchildren. Dan resides with his wife Bonnadeen, in Huntley, Illinois.

...

CPSIA information can be obtained at www.ICGtesting.com
224547LV00001B/1/P